The First

The 16th Donut Mystery

From *New York Times* Bestselling Author

Jessica Beck

BAD BITES

Other Books by Jessica Beck

The Donut Shop Mysteries

Glazed Murder
Fatally Frosted
Sinister Sprinkles
Evil Éclairs
Tragic Toppings
Killer Crullers
Drop Dead Chocolate
Powdered Peril
Illegally Iced
Deadly Donuts
Assault and Batter
Sweet Suspects
Cinnamon Sins
Deep Fried Homicide
Custard Crime
Lemon Larceny
Bad Bites

The Classic Diner Mysteries

A Chili Death
A Deadly Beef
A Killer Cake
A Baked Ham
A Bad Egg
A Real Pickle
A Burned Out Baker

The Ghost Cat Cozy Mysteries

Ghost Cat: Midnight Paws
Ghost Cat 2: Bid for Midnight

Jessica Beck is the *New York Times* Bestselling Author of the Donut Shop Mysteries, the Classic Diner Mysteries, and the Ghost Cat Cozy Mysteries.

To P and E,
For always and forever!

BAD BITES by Jessica Beck; Copyright © 2014

Chapter 1

While there is rarely any true dignity to be found in murder, this homicide offered less than most.

In many ways, it was unfortunate that the victim had been slain dressed from head to toe in a clown outfit, from his floppy shoes to his bright-orange fright wig; the scene was surreal enough without the oversized kitchen knife protruding from his chest. At first glance, it almost appeared to be just another costume prop, but the blood surrounding the wound was brown and uneven, dampening some of the vividly bright colors of the costume, and certainly not the fake bright-red stuff normally expected from a staged scene.

This was where the reality of it all became apparent.

Clearly, this clown had breathed his last, and little did I know at the time how much one death would change my life in so many ways, good and bad, forever.

"Come on, Jake. We need to go right now, or we're going to be late for the party," I told my state policeman/boyfriend as he finished tying his shoes.

It still felt silly to me thinking of this grown man before me as my boyfriend. Somehow that term felt better suited to teenagers, and while neither Jake nor I were exactly old, it had been a few decades since either one of us had attended a high-school dance. Did they even hold them anymore these days?

"Hang on a second. I'm coming," Jake said as he stood up and straightened his tie. "Suzanne, I still can't believe that I'm wasting my one free weekend a month going to a party instead of taking you someplace nice for dinner."

"The library basement is nice enough," I said, "and don't forget, they've got a buffet, too."

Jake looked at me skeptically. "Maybe so, but I'm willing to bet that it isn't as nice as Napoli's, no matter how much money they've shelled out for this party."

We both loved the Italian food the DeAngelis clan served at Napoli's Italian Restaurant, and it was our custom to go there every chance we got, but these were unusual circumstances. "Jake, you know that the police chief's brother is retiring after thirty years spent working at the library. We really *have* to go." Ever since Momma had married the April Springs chief of police, his life had become intertwined with ours, and my mother and I had always believed that in the end, family was the most important thing of all.

"Fine, but you still owe me a dinner at Napoli's, and I mean sooner rather than later," Jake cautioned.

"I promise," I said as I finally herded him out the front door. Jake had put up a smidgeon of resistance when I'd insisted that he stay with me at the cottage on his first visit back to April Springs after he'd spent so much time recovering there, but I'd quickly nixed the idea of him staying anywhere else. After all, we were two consenting adults, and quite frankly, it was nobody's business *where* he stayed when he visited me. What we did or didn't do while he was there was equally off the table, and I pitied anybody who ever found the nerve to ask me directly about our arrangements when my boyfriend was in town.

"It's a nice evening. Should we walk?" Jake asked me as we stood on the porch.

"You're not fooling me, mister. It's clear that you're just stalling."

"Are you saying that you *don't* think it's nice out?" he asked me with a ready smile.

I took a deep breath, grinned back at him, and then I said, "On any other evening, I'd love nothing better than take a stroll with you through the park to the library, but we're going to be late as it is. We'd better take my Jeep."

Jake grumbled a little, but he got in the passenger side, and I drove us the short distance from the cottage to the library.

"What's this man's name again?" he asked me. When he was on a case, he could remember the slightest bit of minutiae, but outside of that, his capacity for recalling names wasn't everything that it should be.

"It's Chester Martin," I said. "I've known him for years, and all in all, he's a pretty good guy. I should warn you about something, though."

"What's that? Does he have a lazy eye, maybe a slight lisp, or is there something else that I need to be aware of?"

"It's nothing quite as subtle as any of that," I said. "Chester loves kids, mostly because he's always been one at heart. I suppose there's a possibility that he might be wearing a suit tonight, but chances are, he'll be dressed as a cowboy or an astronaut instead."

"You're kidding me, right?" Jake asked me as I pulled into the crowded library parking lot.

"Unfortunately, no. Let's just say that Chester's a little eccentric and leave it at that."

"Okay, let's just say that," Jake replied in that calm,

measured tone he used when he was processing new information. I'd had the privilege to see him at work a few times in the past, and they had really been eye-opening experiences for me. Jake was awfully good at what he did, though I had a feeling that lately he'd been growing tired of the high pressure of his job as a state police inspector. It was totally understandable, as far as I was concerned. The cases he got were the tough ones that no one else could crack, and it definitely wore on him at times.

"I suppose we should go wish Chester well," Jake said as he got out of the Jeep and waited for me before we both walked toward the basement door.

"It will be fun. You'll see." I was afraid that we were going to be late, but that turned out not to be an issue after all.

Once we were inside, it appeared that the guest of honor was even later than we were.

"What's going on?" I asked Momma as I spotted her standing near her new husband just inside the library basement door. It was still hard for me to believe that she was married again, but since the wedding, she hadn't seemed so happy in years, so I decided to do my best to embrace the chief as enthusiastically as I could.

"Chester is late, as usual," Momma said with a smile after she kissed my cheek and smiled brightly at Jake.

"No worries. I'm going to go get him in a second," the chief said as he glanced at his watch. "Hey, Jake. Glad to see you. It's really good of you to come," he said as the two men shook hands formally.

"Are you kidding? I wouldn't have missed this for the world," Jake said, and to my surprise, he actually sounded sincere. "Would you like some company rounding him up?" Jake asked the chief.

"Tell you what. Why don't Momma and I go check on him, and you two can catch up," I offered. "He's probably just off in some corner canoodling with Shelly Graham. If he is, then we'll find them both." The chief had been wanting to talk to Jake about something for quite some time, and when he found out that my boyfriend would be visiting again soon, he'd made me promise to make it happen.

The things we do for family, right?

Anyway, this was an easy request to comply with, though the flickering moment of the hurt feelings in Jake's eyes when I'd suggested it told me that I'd have a few fences to mend once this was over. That was okay. I never minded making up with Jake. As a matter of fact, quite often it was half the fun of arguing.

"Who's this 'Shelly'?" Jake asked Chief Martin before Momma and I could get away.

"She's been Chester's girlfriend for quite a while now. She owns a lodge in the mountains, but she's here a lot, especially since she started seeing my brother," the chief explained. "Frankly, I don't see the appeal of it for either one of them, but who knows? Anyway, Shelly's not here yet, either. She called me ten minutes ago and told me to tell Chester that she was running late. Evidently she's having a problem with one of her guests at the lodge."

"Why didn't she call Chester and tell him herself?" Momma asked.

Chief Martin just shrugged. "She claims that she did, but that he's not answering his phone. I can attest to that much myself. I called him two minutes ago, but he wouldn't pick up for me, either."

"Don't worry. We'll track him down. Come on, Momma," I said as I tugged on my mother's arm. I was a good fifty pounds heavier and at least seven inches taller than my mother was, but moving her was going to require some cooperation on her part. What the woman lacked in stature she more than made up for with a solid presence that could stop a bull in mid-charge, not that any sane bull would ever be foolish enough to challenge her.

"We'll be right back," my mother said to her husband, and then she turned to me. "Suzanne, we don't have far to go. Chester must be upstairs in the main part of the library. At least that's where he's supposed to be."

Momma and I walked up the steps together and entered the main floor of the building. I'd expected it to be well lit, but only the emergency lights were on upstairs.

"Chester, it's Dot and Suzanne," my mother called out. "Are you decent?"

There was no response.

"Chester!" Momma repeated, quite a bit louder this time.

"Maybe he's not here," I told her.

"Perhaps," Momma answered, but instead of going back to rejoin the others in the basement, she headed up the narrow staircase to the second-floor offices that overlooked the rest of the library.

"I've never been up here before," I told Momma as we climbed the steps.

"We have our board meetings in the conference room here every month," Momma said. I'd forgotten that she served on the library board, since she participated in so many civic activities around town.

"How do you find the time to do so many different things in April Springs?" I asked her as we approached a closed door at the landing on the top floor. "I run the donut shop seven days a week, and I barely have time for a life outside of that at all."

"The secret is that I never promise too much to any one group," Momma said with a smile, and then she turned and rapped loudly on the door. "Chester! You're missing your own party!"

It would have awakened anyone but the deepest sleeper, but there was still no response.

"I'm telling you, I don't think he's here," I said as I tried the door handle and found that it was locked.

"Nonsense. Where else would he be tonight of all nights?"

Momma reached into her purse and pulled out a key.

"They actually gave you a key to the place?" I asked her as she started to unlock the door.

"Why else do you think I'd ever agree to serve on their board?" she asked with the hint of a smile. "What if I want something to read and it's late at night when the library is closed?"

"You could always just download a book on your e-reader, like most normal folks do," I said.

"I could, but think of what fun I'd miss out on here if I did that. Suzanne, you haven't lived until you've browsed through these stacks alone long after everyone else has gone home."

It sounded like fun at that. "The next time you do it, call me so I can come, too," I said.

"It would be my pleasure," Momma said, and then

she turned the key and opened the door.

The room was quite dark, but that ended the moment I reached out and flicked on the light switch. There is still a part of me that wished I'd left that switch turned off.

Looking down at the floor, we saw Chester Martin, the never-to-fully-retire librarian, replete in his clown outfit, a knife sticking straight up from his chest, and without a doubt, most sincerely and positively dead.

Chapter 2

"Go get Jake and Phillip," Momma said as she knelt down and felt for a pulse despite the obvious state of the murder victim.

"Shouldn't I stay with you?" I asked, unable to tear my gaze away from the brightly clad body and the knife plunged into it.

"Go, Suzanne! We might not be too late!"

I realized beyond all shadow of doubt that we were, but Momma didn't have to tell me again. I rushed down both sets of stairs in record time, though I tried to look calm when I reached the milling guests waiting in vain for the guest of honor to appear. There must have been something in my expression, though, because Jake and the chief both hurried toward me the second they saw me.

"Momma needs you upstairs," I said firmly.

"I'm on my way," Chief Martin said.

"She wants both of you," I explained.

Jake raised an eyebrow, but he didn't say a word, and in less than a second, the two men complied by hurrying up the stairs.

I was about to join them when Gabby Williams cornered me before I could get away, too.

"What's going on, Suzanne? Where on earth is Chester? Is he upstairs waiting to make some kind of grand entrance? What's the fool dressed up as this time, a snake charmer?"

"Hi, Gabby," I said, ignoring every question she'd just pummeled me with. "How's your evening going?"

Gabby snorted. "I doubt you care to hear my honest

answer, and we both know it, so let's dispense with the formalities, shall we? Why am I not surprised that you're defending this kind of behavior?"

"What do you mean by that?"

She snorted a little. "It's clear, isn't it? You two are family now. If there's one thing I know about the Harts, it's their blind loyalty to each other, even when it flies in the face of all reason."

I smiled at her, an act that clearly puzzled her. "Why, Gabby, that's the sweetest thing you've ever said to me."

"Suzanne, it wasn't meant to be a compliment," she snapped.

"And yet that's exactly how I'm going to choose to take it," I said as I finally managed to free myself from her and head up the stairs.

"Hold on a second," someone else commanded before I could escape, but this was a person I would be more than happy to speak with in normal circumstances.

"Hi, Mr. Mayor. I'd love to stay and chat, but something's going on upstairs," I said in a low voice.

"You don't have to tell me that; I knew it the second I saw your face. Don't forget, I was a police officer a lot longer than I've been mayor. Now, what exactly is going on?"

I knew that I might be okay avoiding Gabby's questions, but I couldn't just duck George's. "It's Chester," I said softly.

"What happened to him?" George asked, his voice kept low in return.

"I'm afraid that he's been murdered," I said quietly.

"What?" George asked, loud enough for several

people to stop talking and turn to stare at the two of us.

"Easy, there, Mr. Mayor," I said calmly as I tried to smile to reassure everyone that nothing was wrong.

"Sorry," George said, much more softly this time. "What happened to him?"

"All I know for sure is that he was stabbed in the chest with a mighty big knife," I said. "Jake and the police chief are up there right now, along with my mother."

"Then the situation is in capable hands," he said. "I should probably say something to everyone gathered here to honor him," George added as he glanced around the room. "Chester's absence is already starting to raise some questions."

"I know. Gabby just about tackled me to keep me from going back upstairs."

"You know, the more that I think about it, that's probably where I should be, too," the mayor said. It was clear that old habits were hard for him to break.

I put a hand on his shoulder to stop him. "George, I think you were right the first time. Don't you think your calming presence is needed more down here than it is upstairs?"

The mayor didn't look very happy about it, but he nodded nevertheless. "So, what do you think? Should I go ahead and make an announcement?"

"I'd hold off on that just yet if I were you," I said. "At the very least, I suspect that whoever is going to investigate this is going to want a complete list of names of everyone who is in attendance tonight."

"Do you think one of these folks did it?" George asked as he looked around the crowded basement room again.

"If I were guessing, I'd say that it's a real possibility. What better alibi could anyone ask for than having forty or so other residents of April Springs vouching for them? Not that it's going to mean much in the end."

"You're thinking that whoever killed Chester upstairs came down here afterwards for an alibi? That's some pretty cool thinking for a murderer."

"Who knows? Maybe they're still in shock from what they did. I can't say. All I know is that someone in an official capacity needs to collect every name they can get."

"You're right. I know one thing: Phillip shouldn't run this investigation himself. If he couldn't investigate his ex-wife's murder, he surely can't look into who might have wanted to see his brother dead."

"He's been through a lot lately," I agreed.

"Do you think Jake would take over if I asked him to do it?" George asked me.

"You can always try, but I doubt that his boss is going to allow it. The man's been complaining about Jake never having enough time ever since he went back on full duty after being shot." My boyfriend had been out of work on medical leave after being wounded by a murder suspect, and if I didn't know any better, I could have sworn that his boss resented the time that he'd been away from his job recuperating. I had a hunch that his superior was going to go ballistic if Jake asked to be loaned to the April Springs police force one more time.

"I could always ask the man myself," George said. "He might listen to me."

"It's worth a shot, if that's what you really want," I replied.

"Can you think of anyone in the world more qualified than Jake to investigate this?" George asked. "Because I know that I can't."

"Present company excluded, you mean, right?" I asked the mayor with the hint of a smile.

"Don't kid yourself. I was pretty good when I was on the job, but Jake is better, and I'm not too vain to admit it." The mayor paused, and then he added, "Go on. I know that you're dying to get upstairs. Don't worry about this crowd. If things start getting unruly, I'll settle them all down."

"Thanks," I said as I kissed his cheek. He might present a gruff exterior to the world, but I knew that there was a kind heart underneath it all no matter how deep it might be buried.

As I walked up the steps, fighting the urge the entire time to take them two at a time, I looked back and saw Gabby moving in to speak with George.

Whatever that man earned as mayor wasn't nearly enough, at least not in my opinion, anyway.

As I closed the first-floor door behind me, I saw flashing lights just outside penetrating the growing evening darkness. Momma was at the door letting the EMTs in, and I nodded brief hellos to them both, since they frequented my donut shop. I worked the kind of hours the service industry could count on, which explained some of the myths about cops and donuts. It also seemed to apply to firefighters, ambulance drivers, and anyone else who had to be out and about in the early morning hours when just about every place else was closed.

"How is it going downstairs?" Momma asked me as

we watched them carry the stretcher upstairs to the conference room.

"I had to tell the mayor what was going on," I said.

"Was that wise?" Momma asked me.

"Since he's the only one down there who could stop a riot if it started, I think so, yes."

There must have been a hint of hurt in my voice at the question, because Momma patted my shoulder gently as she said, "Of course. You were absolutely right to tell him. This is just all such a tragedy."

"How's your husband taking it?" I asked. I still couldn't bring myself to call him by his given name, and "Chief Martin" sounded a little too formal for the situation.

"I don't really know. He asked to be alone," Momma said, the hurt obvious in her voice.

"Try not to take it too personally," I said as I touched her shoulder gently. "The man's been through a lot lately."

"I know that. I just wish that he would lean on me a little more for support."

"I'm sure it's just that old habits die hard," I said. "After all, he couldn't count on anyone but himself for years. It's got to be tough asking for help now."

"He doesn't have to ask; I want to freely give it. I'm his wife, for goodness' sake."

"And there's not a happier soul in the world about that fact than him," I said. A troubling thought crossed my mind based on my conversation with George earlier about who would investigate this murder. "He's not trying to run this investigation himself, is he?"

"Right now he and Jake seem to be tiptoeing around jurisdiction," Momma said. "If it weren't all so very tragic, it might be funny how careful they are both being about who should be in charge of this case. Obviously Jake needs to do it, but I can't see telling Phillip that."

"Should I give it a try?" While the chief and I had experienced our differences in the past, I might be able to get through to him.

Momma patted my shoulder as she said, "Thank you for offering, Suzanne. I may take you up on it if I have to later, but for now, let's both just stay out of it and see how it plays out."

A minute later, Jake walked down the second-floor steps and joined us. I'd half expected to see the police chief with him, but my boyfriend was alone.

"Where is Phillip?" Momma asked him.

"I tried to get him to leave the crime scene, but he just wouldn't do it. He wanted to stay with the body," Jake said. "He'd like you to join him, if you wouldn't mind."

"Of course I don't mind. By my husband's side is where I belong."

As Momma hurried up the stairs, I asked Jake, "How's he doing?"

"Not good. The man's a real mess, not that I can blame him. There's no way that he's going to be able to work this murder."

"Are you going to do it?"

Jake just shrugged. "All I can do is ask, which I'm about to do right now. Wish me luck."

"Good luck," I said as Jake pulled out his phone and dialed.

"Hey, Boss. I'm in April Springs, and there's a situation." After Jake explained what had happened, there was a long pause on his end before he spoke again. "It's his brother. Nobody could ask him to do it himself. It's just not right, and besides, there's a precedent that's already been set." After another pause, Jake added, this time a little testily, "As you've pointed out in the past yourself, because of my connections here, nobody's more qualified to investigate this crime than I am." This pause was shorter, but there was real anger in Jake's voice the next time he spoke. "Fine. If that's how it has to be, then I quit. No, I'm not bluffing. You'll get my paperwork in the morning, but as of right now, I'm through."

Then he hung up.

"Jake, did you just quit your job, or were you bluffing despite what you just told your boss?" I asked as he hung up his cell phone.

"Suzanne, you should know me well enough by now to know that I don't bluff. No, I'm done. There's no going back now."

"Come on, Jake. You shouldn't make a rash decision like this without at least giving it some thought."

He took my hands in his as he answered, "Suzanne, ever since I took that bullet, thinking about quitting is just about all that I've done. I've grown too tired and too cynical to keep going, so I need to get out while I still can." He smiled at me before he added, "Hey, I thought you'd be happy about my decision."

"If it's what you truly want, then I am overjoyed about the news. I just don't want you to do it for the wrong reasons."

"Even if one of them is to be closer to you?" he asked me softly.

I felt myself melt a little, but I had to stay strong.

"Even then. Not that I don't love the idea of you being around more, but I know how much your job means to you, how much it defines you."

"You mean even more to me, though," he said.

"Trust me; I don't want to end up like Chester, dying on the day that he retired. Think about how much he missed out on."

"Hang on a second, Jake. You've got a problem," I said with a frown.

"You mean besides the sudden loss of income that I'm about to face? Don't worry. I've saved my nickels and dimes over the years, so you won't have to support me before I find something else."

"You know that you are more than welcome to stay with me and eat at my table for as long as you want to, but that's not what I'm talking about. If you're not a state police inspector anymore, how are you going to have the authority to investigate *anything*?"

Jake frowned as he considered the ramifications of his recent action. "To be honest with you, I hadn't really thought about that."

"Give me a second. I can make this all work out," I said.

I hurried down the steps and found George Morris blocking the door. "Mayor, I need you upstairs for a second," I said.

"I'm happy to help, but what do I do about them?"

I looked around and saw several folks milling about, all of them looking expectantly toward the door waiting for the guest of honor to appear. It was sheer luck that I saw a police officer I knew well just walking in with his date, who just happened to be my best friend, Grace Gauge. She was also my investigating partner, and I had a feeling that I'd need her assistance before this was all over, but for now, I needed her date. I waved, and they both headed toward me.

Once he was there, I said softly, "Officer Grant, there's been a murder upstairs. The victim is the chief's brother, Chester. Can you keep everyone down here until someone gets back to you with further instructions?"

"Mayor?" Officer Grant asked, knowing that I had no authority to make the request, but that his boss's boss did.

"Do as she asks, Officer," George said.

"Yes, sir," he said smartly. I half expected him to salute, but if he felt the urge, he managed to restrain himself.

"Suzanne, do you need me for anything?" Grace asked.

"Not at the moment, but don't go anywhere," I said as George and I made our way upstairs.

"Don't worry. You know me; I'm not going anywhere," she said.

We found Jake standing by the front door, looking as though what he'd done so rashly had finally started to sink in. I'd briefed George about the situation, and the moment he saw Jake, he took over. "Inspector Bishop, the town of April Springs would like to hire you as its Interim Police Chief. I understand that you're looking for work. Are you interested in the position?"

"I'll do it on two conditions," Jake said carefully after a moment.

"I'm sure that we can accommodate your requests,"

George said, slightly taken aback by Jake's tone of voice. "What are they?"

"I want it perfectly clear from the very start that this position is only temporary, no matter what might happen. Once this case is over, I'm relinquishing the post."

It was an odd demand, especially since we already had a full-time chief of police, but George nodded anyway. "Understood. What's your second condition?"

"I won't wear a uniform. I'll carry a badge and a gun, but that's as far as I'm willing to go."

"I don't see a problem with that, either," the mayor responded.

"Then I accept your offer," Jake said as he shook George's hand.

Momma and the chief must have been listening at the top of the steps, because they walked down and joined us. "The whole job is yours forever if you want it," Chief Martin said grimly. "I'm done. Seeing my brother cut down like that on the day of his retirement is more than a man should have to deal with. I won't risk another day on this job if I don't have to, and fortunately, I don't have to."

Momma patted his shoulder. "There's no reason why you should, Phillip. You've served this town well. Now it's someone else's turn."

"Just as long as it's not mine," Jake said. "I'll hang around until you can find somebody else on a permanent basis, but you're not the only one retiring from police work. I just quit, myself."

"Jake, are you certain about that decision?" my mother asked him carefully.

"I've never been more sure of anything in my life," he said confidently.

"Then congratulations are in order."

Jake smiled for a moment before it disappeared. "Thanks, but I want everyone to remember that I'm just here long enough to catch one killer."

"That's all that matters to me," the chief said, and then, to my surprise, he handed Jake his badge. "Find whoever killed my brother, Jake."

"That's what I intend to do," my boyfriend said as he slid the badge into his front pocket.

A thought suddenly occurred to me. "Has anyone told Shelly? Shouldn't she have been here by now?"

"She knows what happened," Momma said. "The poor woman was a wreck when I told her a few moments after she got here. Luckily a friend was here with her for the party, so she could take her home. I'm just glad that she's got someone to stay with her."

"The mayor asked Officer Grant to keep everyone downstairs," I reported to Jake. "He's down there awaiting further orders."

"Good, because he's going to get them," Jake said as he started for the steps.

"Do you need any backup down there?" George asked him, a question that I had been about to ask myself.

"Not at the moment, but I might need you later," he said. Jake barely looked at me as he left the room, and I knew that he was already in full investigative mode. Turning back to the former chief, Jake said, "Don't let anyone touch anything upstairs until that scene has been searched and filmed, and that includes moving the body once they determine for sure that the victim is dead. Chief, I know that you're finished with police work, but I need you for another hour before you hang it up for good. Can you do that for me?"

"For my brother I can," the chief said. "I've got a full crime-scene kit in the trunk of my car, so I can do it myself," Chief Martin said, and then he left for the parking lot.

"Is that wise, Jake?" Momma asked him after her new husband was gone.

"Don't worry. I'll have someone else handle the actual evidence gathering. Getting the kit will at least give him something to do." Jake turned to the mayor as he asked, "Can you get someone else over here to take care of that?"

"I can, and I will," George said.

"Good. Now if you'll all excuse me, I've got work to do," Jake said as he left us as well.

Now it was just down to Momma and me.

"You're going to look into this murder yourself, aren't you, Suzanne?" my mother asked me softly, even though we were now alone.

"Why do you want to know? Are you volunteering to lend me a hand?"

"No, that was a one-time experience for me," she said. Momma had indeed been a great help in an earlier investigation, but she'd also expressed to me just how much she'd never wanted to do it again. "I'm sure that Grace would be delighted to assist you."

"She's already offered her services," I said, "but I'm sure that Jake can handle this without either one of us."

"Perhaps, but I'm just as certain that he could still use your help. After all, no one knows April Springs better than you do."

"Unless maybe it's you," I said.

"As I said, I'm not interested, but even if I were, I'm not sure that I agree with you anymore. Your donut shop gives you a reach into the community that I've always lacked. Use every resource you have to find this killer, Suzanne. My husband needs the peace that only that will bring."

"Grace and I will do our best to lend a hand, but only if Jake approves," I said. It was, in the end, all that I could promise her, no matter how much I wanted to please her. I wasn't about to tromp all over my boyfriend's investigation if he didn't want me meddling in it. Then again, I'd provided a few valuable bits of information in the past, and I was hoping that I could do it again with this case.

"See to it that he does, then," Momma said sternly.

"All I can do is ask him."

"You can do a great deal more than that, and we both know it."

"Okay then, I'll ask him strongly," I said with a slight grin.

"That's my girl," Momma said as her husband returned. She left me to speak with him in whispers, and I suddenly felt as though I didn't belong in the room with them.

I decided that it was time to head downstairs to see how Jake was doing with his new job and his brand new title, too.

Chapter 3

"People, may I have your attention?" I heard Jake ask from the stage. Most folks in town knew who he was, but even if they didn't, his commanding tone of voice would have gotten their compliance anyway. Officer Stephen Grant stood beside him on the platform, lending him more authority as well. After the folks gathered in the basement were listening, Jake continued. "I'm afraid that I've got some bad news for you. Our guest of honor, Chester Martin, was murdered this evening."

For a split second, the crowd was stunned into silence, but that didn't last long. Jake was suddenly hammered with questions from the audience before he could say another word. If I didn't know better, I would have sworn that there were at least a hundred people gathered there based on how loud they were being. It reminded me of the time I'd foolhardily volunteered at the elementary school during their lunch hour. After I left there, I had a headache for three days that no pain reliever in the world could touch from the constant din those kids could produce.

"Everybody needs to quiet down," Officer Grant said, and to my surprise, they all listened.

Jake nodded to him in thanks, and then he continued. "I understand that you all have a great many questions right now, but I'm afraid that we don't have many answers, at least not yet, but we will; you can count on that."

"Why are you the one telling us and not Chief Martin?" Ray Blake wanted to know. "After all, he was the man's own brother." Ray ran the town's only newspaper, but of more significance to me was that he was my assistant Emma Blake's father. Ray could be a considerable thorn in my side, but Emma loved the man dearly, so I had to tread lightly whenever I was around him.

"Naturally, the chief has recused himself from the case, given his relationship with the victim. Mayor Morris has asked me to step in during the interim to investigate, and I've agreed."

"What about your job as a state police inspector?" Ray asked. "Have they given you permission to leave again?" Leave it to Ray to ask that particular question.

"I'm not responding to any inquiries right now, from the press or anyone else," Jake said, icing the newspaperman with his stare. "I'm the one looking for answers, and I need you all to be patient with me. Officer Grant will be stationed at the door, and he'll take your names as you file out the door. If he doesn't know you by sight, be prepared to show him some kind of identification. That's all for now."

That wasn't the end of it, though.

"How did he die?"

"When exactly did it happen?"

"Do you have any suspects yet?"

The questions continued to ring out, but they might as well have been whispers in a hurricane for all the impact they had on Jake. I saw him lean forward to say something to Officer Grant, who then quickly moved into position by the door, his notepad ready down to take every name.

A few folks, including Ray, didn't get the hint, and they wouldn't leave Jake alone.

"I'm sorry, but I don't have more for you at this time," Jake kept repeating.

"You can't ignore the press," Ray said as he muscled his way closer to Jake.

"You're right," Jake said. "What's your first question?"

"How exactly was the victim murdered?" Ray asked eagerly.

"No comment," Jake replied.

"Who found the body?"

"No comment," Jake repeated.

"What time was the victim discovered?" Ray asked doggedly.

"No comment. Are you sensing a trend here, Ray?" Jake asked him.

The newspaperman slapped his notebook shut. "I'll get the answers, if not from you, then from someone else."

"Just don't interfere with my investigation," Jake said softly, and I swore that I saw Ray flinch a little.

"Is that a threat, Inspector?"

"It's Chief, and you should just consider it a bit of friendly advice," Jake said.

"We'll see about that," Ray replied as he moved over to Officer Grant.

"I don't think he likes you very much," I told Jake with a smile as I approached him.

"Imagine my surprise. I'll try to do my best to contain my disappointment," Jake replied.

"Listen, I know that you're busy, but do you have a second? I wouldn't ask if it weren't important."

Jake frowned for a moment, and then he said, "Let me guess. Your mother has asked you to investigate

Chester's murder too, hasn't she?"

"How could you possibly know that?" I asked him.

"Hey, I'm a former state police inspector, remember?" he asked me with the hint of a smile.

"Do you mind? I promise that we'll stay on the perimeter of your investigation, but there might be things we can uncover that you might not be able to find out officially."

Jake frowned again for a full three seconds, and then he finally said, "I don't suppose it would do any good to ask you to let me handle this by myself, would it?"

I took a deep breath, and then I let it out slowly before I spoke again. "Jake, if you are dead set against me investigating this, I'll butt out. You have my word." It was important for me to please my mother, but it was even more crucial that I didn't go against Jake's wishes without good cause.

He appeared to consider that for a few more beats, and then he shrugged. "Why not? After all, it's true. You know the players around here better than I do, so you might have some useful insights. Just don't take any unnecessary chances, okay? Have you spoken with Grace about helping you? I'd feel a lot better about this if she were working alongside you."

"Grace is always eager to help," I admitted, "contingent on your approval, of course."

"Of course," he said with a wry grin. "So, do you have any suspects for me yet?"

"I've already given it a little thought, and I can think of two or three people right off the bat who might have wanted to kill Chester," I said.

Jake studied me for a moment before he spoke. "Are you serious? Who would want to kill a librarian?"

"More folks than you might imagine. Would you like a rundown of them right now?"

"It might be helpful," Jake said, and then we both heard a ruckus at the door where folks were filing past Officer Grant. "Maybe later, okay? I'd better go see what's going on."

"Sure thing, Chief," I said with the hint of a smile.

"Interim Chief," he corrected me.

"Sorry, but that's just too clunky for me to say."

Jake didn't answer as he hurried over to see what the commotion was about.

I hadn't seen Grace standing off to one side, but she quickly joined me as Jake left my side.

"I wonder what that's all about?" Grace asked me.

"It appears that Vince Dade has a problem with authority," I said. "Maybe it's because he's got to be on every suspect list that's being created right now."

"There was certainly never any love lost between him and Chester while the man was alive," Grace said. "How could he possibly think that he's helping his case right now by making a scene?"

"I've got a hunch that he's not thinking all that clearly," I said as I saw Jake clamp a hand down on Vince's shoulder. The man winced under the pressure Jake was applying, and his voice lowered almost immediately.

"Suzanne, you've got to hand it to your boyfriend. That's some good crowd-control skills he has going on there."

"Among other things," I said. "By the way, he's agreed to let us investigate on the side, if you're up for it. What do you say?"

"Do you even have to ask?"

"I don't know. I thought that I should," I said.

"Of course I'm all in. This has to be hard on your new stepdad."

"I'm sure that it is," I said, "but Momma's the one I'm worried about. She's concerned about what this might do to her husband, so I promised her that we'd do what we could to help."

"Where should we get started?" Grace asked.

"Let's go somewhere quiet and make a list of anyone we can come up with who might have wanted Chester dead and why."

"That's as good a place to start as any. Should we head over to your house to do it?"

I considered it, but what if Jake came in while we were still working? I'd promised to share my thoughts with him, but I suddenly realized that I wasn't anywhere close to being ready for that yet. "Can we do it at your place instead?"

"Of course we can," Grace said. "Do you need a lift?"

"Thanks, but I drove over here, so my Jeep's outside," I said.

"Then I'll meet you at home—my home, that is."

I tried to tell Jake where I was going, but he'd pulled Vince over to one side and was having a solemn talk with him, so I knew better than to interrupt him.

After Grace and I nodded to Officer Grant, he told her, "Sorry about all of this. May I call you later?"

"Hey, duty called. I understand. Sure, touch base whenever you get a chance."

"How's that going?" I asked Grace as we left him and started outside together.

"Good, but we're still taking things slowly."

"There's nothing wrong with that," I said.

"Said the woman who's been dating a grown man forever without committing one way or the other," Grace replied with a smile.

"What can I say? It's complicated."

"It always is, isn't it?" she asked. "What about that trip to Paris you were going to take together?"

"We still want to go, but Jake hasn't been able to get the time off," I said.

"Well, now that he's quit, that's not going to be a problem anymore, is it?"

I suddenly realized that Grace was right. "After Chester's killer is found, we're going. End of discussion."

Our conversation ended as we went outside and joined the milling crowd. Most of the folks who'd come to celebrate Chester's retirement were still there, and I suddenly realized that it might be the perfect time to question a few folks while they were a little more receptive than they might be later.

"Ladies, isn't it all just horrific?" Zelda Marks asked as she approached us. Zelda had been, up until the moment that he'd been murdered, Chester Martin's assistant librarian. Upon Chester's official resignation at midnight, Zelda was due to take over. This was a perfect resource for our investigation because she knew Chester better than anyone else in April Springs, including the police chief.

"It's terrible what happened," I said sympathetically. "Can you imagine who would want to hurt Chester?"

Zelda frowned a bit as I asked the question, but she quickly concealed it. Grace must have caught it, too, though, based on her next question.

"Do you have any thoughts about it, Zelda?" Grace asked her.

"I really couldn't say," she said dismissively.

In my most earnest voice, I said, "Everyone knows that you two didn't just work together; you were the best of friends. Surely you want to see Chester's killer brought to justice as much as anyone else does."

It looked as though Zelda was about to cry, and for a second I felt sorry for pushing her, but as unfortunate as the timing of it was, it happened that way sometimes. Grace started to add something, but I shook my head slightly, and she picked up on my hint and kept quiet.

After a few moments of silence, Zelda said as she looked around, "I wouldn't mind helping you, but it doesn't feel right talking about it here, so close to where it happened." She looked around at the other folks still gathered together, and I had to wonder if any of her suspects were still present, and that was the real reason she was being so reticent to talk to us.

"We don't have to do it in the parking lot," Grace said. "Suzanne and I were about to go back to my place for some coffee. Would you care to join us?"

I'd wanted to stay and talk to a few other potential sources of information, but Grace was right. Zelda might be the mother lode, and if we wanted the real scoop on Chester's enemies, there was no one better to speak with.

"Well, I *could* use a ride home," Zelda said hesitantly.

"I'll take you myself after we've had a cup and our little chat," Grace said warmly. "Suzanne, why don't you ride in the backseat so Zelda can sit up front with me?"

I'd planned on driving over to her place in my Jeep, but Grace's suggestion made sense. It might put Zelda more at ease if we all rode over together, and I could always pick my Jeep up later. "That sounds great." "Let's go then, shall we?"

"There's just one problem," Zelda said, and I wondered what was about to go wrong. As I waited to hear her complaint, the new head librarian surprised me by saying, "I don't drink coffee."

I felt the relief flow through me that it was something so simple. "How about hot chocolate instead? There's a nip in the air this evening, so it might be a nice change of pace."

"That would be lovely," Zelda said. "Are you certain that you don't mind?"

"Not at all. It would be our pleasure," Grace said.

I just hoped that my best friend had some hot chocolate at her place, but if she didn't, it was a short walk up the road to my cottage to retrieve some. When Momma and I had lived there together up until lately, we'd been known to make up a batch of hot cocoa and sit outside, no matter how chilly it might be. I missed those special times that I'd spent with her, but I knew that she was much happier living across town with her new husband now.

When we got to Grace's house, she walked through the place flipping on lights on her way to the kitchen. "I'll start some milk warming on the stove."

"Excellent," I said. "In the meantime, may I take your coat, Zelda?"

"That would be lovely," the new head librarian said as she handed it to me.

After we both sat in the living room, I said, "You

reacted oddly when I asked you who might have wanted to harm Chester."

"I'm sure that I don't know what you are talking about," Zelda said, refusing to make eye contact with me as she spoke.

"It's okay to talk to us," I said in a calm, reassuring voice. "You're among friends. Besides, Grace and I have done this kind of thing before. We can honestly help, if you'll just let us."

"Oh, you don't have to tell me. I've heard the rumors about your exploits," Zelda said. "After all, folks in April Springs do tend to talk. There's nothing official about your investigation, though, is there?"

"Well, it might help you to know that the interim police chief has approved of us conducting our own investigation, as long as it doesn't interfere with what he's doing."

Zelda looked a little unsure about that. "Does that mean that you'll run and tell him everything that I say?"

"That depends," I answered truthfully. "If that possibility is a problem for you, then maybe you shouldn't talk to us after all."

Grace chose that moment to walk in and join us, and I had to wonder if she'd been listening in from the kitchen all along. And why wouldn't she be eavesdropping? I would have done the same thing myself if our roles had been reversed. "Zelda," she asked, "what if we promise to talk to you before we share what you tell us with anyone else, including Jake? You can trust us to be discreet."

"How can I be sure of that?" the librarian asked.

"Well, have you ever heard *anyone* claim that we

weren't?" Grace asked her. "Surely in your official capacity you hear a great deal of gossip."

"People do like to talk, even in libraries," she said.

"There you go. You must know that you can trust us."

"Very well," she said after letting out a sigh of breath. "Besides, I have to tell someone. Maybe it would be better if I just share all that I know with you, and then let you two decide what the best course of action is for me. I've read a thousand mysteries in my life, but this is real, and I'm beside myself as to what I should do next."

The timer in the kitchen went off, and Grace stood quickly. "Don't start without me. I need one minute."

"May we give you a hand?" I asked.

"No, I've got it."

Zelda and I tried to make a little small talk about the weather while we waited for Grace, but it quickly fizzled out. I wanted to get started with the interview, but one minute hadn't seemed that long to wait.

Apparently, I was wrong. It was taking forever.

Finally, Grace appeared with a tray. It held three cups and saucers, along with plates and a nice selection of cookies. "I thought that we all might be able to use a bite, since the buffet was canceled."

Zelda nodded her thanks as Grace handed her a cup. She took a sip before I could get mine, and she made a contented little sound. "That's absolutely wonderful."

"It's Suzanne's special blend," Grace admitted. "I don't know what she puts in it, but it beats anything you can find in a grocery store."

"We can trade recipes later," I said impatiently. "Let's talk about Chester." I turned to Zelda as I continued, "Now, do you know anyone who might want to see Chester dead?"

"Actually, I know of three people. It's shocking when I say it out loud, isn't it? Who could imagine that a small-town librarian could raise such malevolence in some folks?"

"It *always* surprises me when anyone commits murder," I said, "and yet they continue to do it. Would you mind telling us the names of the three people you're talking about, and why exactly they might want to kill your former boss?"

Chapter 4

"I feel like some kind of informant telling you both this, but someone needs to know the truth," Zelda said as she looked earnestly from me to Grace and then back again. "Ladies, it's important to me that you know that I'm not a gossip. I don't believe in spreading rumors."

"They aren't rumors if we don't tell anyone else," I said, doing my best to reassure her. "Zelda, you could be the only link between Chester and whoever killed him. If you keep silent, the murderer might get away with it, and I know that you don't want that."

"Of course I don't," she said forcefully.

"Then tell us what you saw, and leave the rest of it up to us," I said.

It was touch and go for a second, but finally, she agreed. "Just because I know that you're right doesn't make it any easier for me, but I understand that I can't keep it to myself any longer. Okay, here goes. First thing this morning when we opened, Vince Dade was there waiting for us. Well, more specifically, he was lying in wait for Chester. Vince started in on him the second I unlocked the door, but Chester insisted that they wait to speak in his office. Vince wasn't happy about it, but Chester insisted. I started restocking books, but I'd been concerned about the tone of their conversation, so I decided to check on them upstairs a little later. As I reached Chester's door, Vince came out, clearly upset about something. Before he left, he paused and turned back to Chester, and then he said in a cold and calculating voice, 'I told you that it's over. I'm done with you, once and for all.' After Vince was gone, I asked Chester if everything was all right, but it was almost as though he didn't hear me at first. The expression on his face was really puzzling, and I had to wonder just what their argument had been about."

"Did you hear anything at all of what it might have been about?" Grace asked her.

"Not a word. As you probably know, the offices are all upstairs, and they are well soundproofed. I was on the main floor below in the stacks, but even if I'd been in the conference room next to Chester's office, I wouldn't have been able to hear a thing. Somebody needs to find out what Vince and Chester were talking about and why Vince was through with him."

"We will, or the new chief of police will take care of that himself," I said. "Who else did you have in mind as a potential killer?"

Zelda bit her lip for a moment, and then she said, "This is rather delicate, so I'm not exactly sure how to say it."

"Just give us the basics, then, and we'll fill in the blanks," Grace said.

Zelda nodded. "Lately, Maggie Hoff has been coming by the library two or three times a week to see my boss. She even came by early this afternoon, and without so much as a wave to me, she went straight to Chester's office with a rather determined look on her face."

"How long did she usually stay when she visited in the past?" I asked her.

"I have no idea. Chester always sent me home as soon as she arrived."

"Maggie's still married to Nathan Hoff, isn't she?" Grace asked.

"She is, but I've heard that he works some nights and weekends now. I'm not saying that Maggie and Chester were having an affair. I want to make that crystal clear."

"Got it," I said, filing that particular little tidbit away for later. I wanted to discuss what it might mean with Grace, but not in front of Zelda.

"That's three," I said.

Zelda looked surprised. "I've just mentioned two people so far."

"Actually, you've talked about three of them. If Maggie and Chester were up to something, it might give Nathan a motive as well."

Zelda frowned. "I never even considered that as a possibility."

"Sorry, but that's just the way my mind works sometimes," I said. "What's the last name on your list?"

"This one I'm sure that you're really not going to like," she said. "I hesitate even telling you now."

"Remember, you don't have anything to be afraid of from us," Grace said.

"Well, if you're sure that it won't be a black mark against me, I suppose that I have to tell you."

I was beginning to wonder if she was ever going to say the name after all when she finally admitted, "Just after Maggie left, Chester had one last visitor, and the two men had a heated argument before my boss actually threw his visitor out."

That sounded like a real possibility to me. "This might be important. Who was it?"

"It was the mayor," Zelda said softly.

"Hang on a second," I said. "Are you telling us that

George Morris had a fight with Chester today? What
could the two of them have possibly been arguing
about?"

"I don't know, but it was pretty intense. I thought
for a second that the mayor was going to snap, and it
wasn't pretty."

I knew that George had a temper, but I couldn't
imagine him killing anyone. He'd been injured once
helping me in one of my past investigations, and it had
nearly destroyed me knowing that he'd been hurt
because of me. Maybe I was biased, but there was no
way that I could see the man as a cold-blooded killer.
Still, I had to talk to him, no matter what my personal
feelings might be.

"What about Shelly Graham?" I asked her, wanting
to see what she had to say about the woman her boss
had been dating.

"What about her?" Zelda asked, keeping her gaze on
her hot chocolate.

"Would she have had any reason to kill Chester?"

Zelda looked surprised by my question. "I can't
imagine it. Why would she?"

"Think about it," Grace said. "If Chester *was* fooling
around with Maggie on the side, some folks might say
that was motive enough."

"Maybe if Maggie was the one who was murdered,
I'd agree with you, but Shelly would never have hurt
Chester. I refuse to believe that."

The librarian sounded so sure of that fact that I
decided not to push her any further about it just yet. I
was about to ask another question when Zelda took one
last sip of her cocoa and put the cup back on the tray.
"I'm sorry, but that's all I've got for you. It's getting

late, and I'm quite tired. Would you mind taking me home now?"

"We'd be happy to," I said as Grace frowned a little. Clearly she wasn't finished questioning the woman, either, but we couldn't exactly hold her there against her will. "Grace, would you mind dropping me off at my Jeep on the way?"

"I'd be happy to, or we could go get it together after we take Zelda home." The implication was clear. Grace knew that I was up to something, and she wanted to be a part of it. Ordinarily, I would have welcomed her presence, but for my talk with George, I knew that I needed to be alone.

"Thanks, but there's something I need to do on my own," I said.

Grace seemed to understand, even if she clearly didn't like it. "Let's all go, then."

"Thanks for the lift," I said as Grace parked near my Jeep. The crowd had finally dispersed, though it was clear that there was still a heavy police presence at the library, even at that late an hour.

"Any time. Call me when you get in tonight, no matter how late it might be."

I glanced at my watch. It was just past eight, but I knew what she meant. It might not be late for most folks, but I was seriously cutting into my sleep. After all, I'd have to be up too soon to start making donuts again, but I was just going to have to deal with being a little sleep deprived tomorrow.

I still had something important to do tonight.

"May I come in?" I asked George as he answered the

46

door.

"Suzanne, isn't this kind of late for you to still be up?"

"Ordinarily it's true, but there's something that we need to talk about, and it can't wait another minute," I said as I stepped past him inside. The mayor lived alone, and it showed, with books and magazines spread out on nearly every horizontal space in the place. I was surprised it wasn't tidier than it was, though, given the fact that he had a girlfriend he saw on a regular basis.

"Excuse the mess, but Polly's out of town again visiting family," George explained.

I knew that his secretary, and his love interest as well, had been spending quite a bit of time out of town with her grandchildren lately. "I'm sure that you miss her when she's gone."

"It's true. Now, what can I do for you?" he asked as he shuffled a few magazines off two chairs and motioned for me to sit down.

There was no use beating around the bush. "I heard that you and Chester Martin had a huge argument this afternoon."

George looked angry when I mentioned it, and it was clear in his tone that he wasn't all that happy about me bringing it up now. "That blasted Zelda Marks couldn't keep her mouth shut if her life depended on it."

"I didn't say that Zelda told me anything," I said.

He looked at me sharply. "If it wasn't her, then who could it possibly have been?"

"George, is that really what's important right now? What I need to know is if it's true."

"It's true," the mayor admitted, clearly disgusted about something.

"What were you two fighting about?" I asked.

"Suzanne, sorry for being rude, but I don't see how that's any of your business."

George could be abrupt to the point of insolence, but I wasn't going to let that stop me from getting an answer to my question. "Maybe not, but even if you don't tell me, what do you think the odds are of me not saying something to Jake?"

"You'd actually betray our friendship that way?" he asked me.

"Hey, if you don't have anything to hide, you're the one who is out of line here. If it's innocent, tell me and I'll drop it, but if it's not, then it's fair game as far as I'm concerned."

"Should I regret hiring Jake as our interim chief?" he asked me with a hint of steel in his voice.

"Not if you want the murderer caught," I said. "Now, are you just being stubborn, or do you have something to hide?"

"Stubborn, I guess," George said as he melted a little. I knew the man well enough to know that it was important to keep my mouth shut at that point. He'd tell me what I wanted to know now. It was just a matter of giving him a little time to come to grips with it. After a full minute, my instincts paid off and George began to explain. "I don't know if you realize it, but Chester and I go way back," he began. "We'd been friends long enough that when he was making a fool of himself, I took it upon myself to call him on it."

"What was he doing that you didn't approve of?" I asked the mayor.

"That was between the two of us," George said stubbornly.

"Need I remind you that you were a cop once upon a time?" I asked him. "Do you think for one second that excuse is going to work with me?"

"Suzanne, you're not a cop," George said. There was a hint of a grin hiding behind his mask, but I chose to ignore it.

"No, but Jake is, and we both know that you aren't going to be able to stonewall him. You might be able to fire him, but there's no way that you're going to tell him what to do."

"That's true enough," George said, and then let out a sigh. "I might as well tell you, then, but it's not going to look good on Chester or me."

"I can deal with that if you can," I said. "All I want is the truth."

"That might be harder to come by than you think," George said.

"Are you seriously trying to stall me? Just tell me," I urged him.

"Fine," George said. "I was there to tell him that he needed to straighten up and get his act together before something bad happened to him."

"I'm guessing that he didn't like you interfering in his life, did he?"

"He lost it, Suzanne. It was bad enough when I told him that he needed to quit cheating on Shelly, but when I said that pushing Vince Dade was going to be the end of him, he started yelling at me to mind my own business."

"So you were just looking out for his best interests, is that it?" I asked the mayor. Knowing George, it was easy enough to imagine that what he was telling me was true. Unfortunately, Zelda had heard the confrontation, and she'd taken something very different from it. True or not, Jake needed to know about it. "I have to tell Jake. You realize that, don't you?"

"I know it all too well. It's going to make me sound like some kind of nut, though."

I touched his shoulder gently. "I don't think that at all. The worst it might do is make you look as though you care."

"Yeah, well, I don't necessarily want it to get around town that I have a sensitive side, you know what I mean?"

Thinking about how gruff the mayor could be, I didn't think that was anything that he was going to have to worry about. "You should be safe enough. Do you have any idea what Chester's problem with Vince Dade was?"

"Are you telling me that you didn't know?" George asked, clearly surprised.

"No, I don't have a clue what you're talking about."

The mayor shrugged. "Now that I think about it, I guess that all happened before your time. Chester, Vince, and a few dozen other investors were business partners on the side about ten years ago. They put together a group that dabbled in land speculation to lure a big hotel complex that was supposed to be coming to the area, but it got too risky for Chester's blood, so he wanted out just before the final agreement was signed. Vince took it upon himself to buy all of Chester's shares and a couple of others too, and a month later, the main part of the land was declared unbuildable. I heard it was due to the ground being unstable or something like that. Anyway, the hotel venture pulled out, and apparently Vince ended up losing his shirt."

"What did that have to do with Chester? I can understand Vince being upset, but it just sounds like bad luck to me. Did Chester or the other two investors have any idea that the land was nearly worthless when they sold their shares back to Vince?"

"Not that I ever heard, but that didn't keep Vince from carrying a grudge all of these years. I'm kind of surprised that your mother didn't tell you about this."

That was an odd thing for him to say. "What does Momma have to do with it?"

"Well, she and her new husband were the other two investors Vince bought out," George explained.

Chapter 5

"Are you serious?"

"Suzanne, you know me well enough to realize that I don't kid around about something like that," George said.

I wanted to rush right over to Momma's to get her side of things, but I wasn't done with my friend yet, so that was just going to have to wait. "George, you've mentioned a few folks who might have wanted Chester dead, people that I've already suspected might have done it. Is there anyone else you can think of that I should check out in my investigation?"

"Kevin Leeds," George said so softly that I had to strain to hear it.

"Kevin? What beef did he have with Chester?"

"I have no idea," the mayor admitted. "All I know is that there's been bad blood between Kevin and Chester for years."

I stood. "Well, thanks for your time, and the explanation."

"There's one more person that you should look for," George said before I could make it out the door.

"Who might that be?" I asked.

"I don't have a name for you, but one thing that I learned when I was a cop was to always consider who had the most to gain by the victim's death."

"Did Chester carry life insurance? Who gets his retirement account now that he's dead?"

"I don't know, but you need to ask Jake about them both."

"Thanks for the tip," I said, not really sure whether

I'd ask my boyfriend that or not. After all, it was too far into his jurisdiction and not enough in mine. I was good at getting folks to admit things they might not to the police, but when it came to seeing restricted records, that was all on Jake. Still, it gave me something to think about. Maybe if the opportunity arose, I'd ask him about it, but I had something far more pressing ahead of me at the moment.

I needed to speak with my mother and her new husband about a land deal that happened over a decade ago and try to figure out if it might have offered enough motive for murder today.

"Do you have a second, Momma?" I asked after my mother answered the door of her new place.

"For you? Always. Come in, Suzanne."

"Thanks," I said as I walked into the living room. The chief, er, the former chief was there, going through an old magazine about Alaska.

"I'll just leave you two alone," he said as he closed the magazine and started to stand.

"Actually, I'd appreciate it if you'd hang around. This concerns you, too."

"Is it about Chester? Did Jake find the killer already?" There was real hope in his voice as he asked, and I hated to disappoint him.

"Not that I know of."

"But this is part of *your* investigation; am I right there?"

"You are."

"Well, Dot and I will do whatever we can in our power to help you," Chief Martin said. "All you have to do is ask." I didn't care about his change in status, or the shift in his demeanor. He'd always be the chief of police to me, even though Jake was currently doing his job, and there was a part of me that liked things the way they had been.

"I'm kind of surprised that you are being so cooperative," I said as I took a seat near the fireplace.

"That's because we're on the same team now," he said. "What can we do for you?"

"I need to know about the land speculation deal you and Momma went in on with Chester and Vince Dade," I said.

"Who told you about that?" my mother asked me.

"Is it important?" I asked. "What happened?"

"It was all such a long time ago," Momma said. "Surely you don't think it's the reason Chester was murdered, do you?"

"Momma, you've seen me work. I usually don't know which clues are significant and which ones aren't until I've figured out the entire puzzle."

She nodded, and the police chief spoke. "I don't mind talking about it. It was going to be big for April Springs, and everyone was trying to figure out where the hotel was going to go. Vince seemed to have the inside track, though he never told us how, so Chester and I decided to invest when he approached us."

"I came in a few days after they did," my mother said. "Vince could be very convincing, and that was before I'd fully developed my keen business senses." Coming from anyone else, it would have sounded a little pretentious, but from Momma, it was simply the truth. My mother frowned for a moment, and then she added, "I'm afraid that I was the cause of Chester pulling out in the first place."

The chief looked surprised to hear that. "What do you mean?"

Momma sat beside him and patted his knee. "Chester didn't want you to know at the time, and I saw no reason to tell you. He came to me, worried that he was going to lose his original investment, so I told him that if he wasn't comfortable with the risk, he should pull out of the deal. I even offered to buy his share, but he told me that he'd rather get it from Vince. I was going to be his fallback plan, but I never had to come through for him. I was startled when Vince offered to buy me out as well when I started asking questions of my own, but I had enough trepidation about the project at that point to accept his offer." She looked over at her husband as she asked, "When did you sell your portion to him?"

"After Chester, but before you," the chief said.

"Did your brother share his concerns with you as well?" Momma asked.

The chief looked uncomfortable as he admitted, "No, it wasn't anything like that. My wife found out what I'd done, so she made me do it. I took a bit of a hit on the investment, but at least it kept a bit of peace in a marriage that had precious little of it at that point."

"So then, Vince didn't have any reason to be mad at you, but he certainly had cause to be angry with me," Momma said.

"That's not entirely true," I said.

"What do you mean?"

"He didn't know that you advised Chester to pull out, did he?"

"I highly doubt it. Chester wasn't one to ask anyone for help or advice, so I doubt that he shared with Vince the fact that he had felt compelled to share his concerns with me."

"Maybe we shouldn't tell Vince about that part of it," Chief Martin said gravely.

"Honestly, you can't seriously think that I'm in danger now because of something that happened ten years ago, can you?" my mother asked her husband incredulously.

"Dot, until we know exactly who killed Chester, and why, I'm going to take everything seriously," he told her. "And I suggest that you both do the same."

"I for one always do," I said as I tried to stifle a yawn.

"Suzanne, you look tired. Isn't it past your bedtime, or have you decided to let Sharon and Emma make the donuts tomorrow?" Momma asked me.

"No, I'm doing it myself," I said as I tried to stop another one. "You're probably right. I'd better go back to the cottage and get some sleep," I added.

"Be careful," Momma said, a sentiment the chief echoed as they walked me to their door.

After I waved good-bye, I headed back to the cottage that Momma and I had shared once upon a time. It seemed like forever now, but it in the grand scheme of things, it hadn't been that long ago at all. Jake was there, at least for now, though it was clear from the lack of vehicles in the driveway that he was still out investigating. A part of me was sad not to be able to kiss him good night, but another part was just as happy that I wouldn't have to explain any of my partially formed theories quite yet. Besides, they weren't all that clear in my own mind. Maybe a good night's sleep would crystallize things for me, but the worst-case scenario was that I would at least get some rest, and that was never a bad thing.

Chapter 6

I'd been hoping that Jake would be there when I got back to the cottage, but a part of me knew that probably wasn't going to happen. The man had an intensity and focus when he was working a case like I'd never seen, and I realized that I'd be lucky if I saw him at all over the course of the next few days and weeks. I checked in with Grace, grabbed a yogurt from the fridge, and then I curled up on the couch, though I probably should have just gone to bed. The problem with that was if I did go upstairs, I'd have zero chance of seeing Jake if and when he made it back to the cottage. If he found me asleep on the couch, there would at least be a chance that he'd wake me.

And that's exactly what happened.

"Suzanne, it's time to get up," I heard him say as he gently shook my shoulder.

"Five more minutes, Momma," I said, still not completely awake.

"I don't know whether I should feel complimented or insulted by that," he said as I sat up and rubbed the sleep from my eyes.

"What time is it?"

"Right on time for you, but too late for me, or too early, whichever way you choose to look at it. Here, have some coffee," he added as he handed me a mug.

"You made this?" I asked as I took a healthy drink and almost choked. It was stout, much stronger than I preferred, but I wasn't about to be a choosy beggar.

"Hey, you've done it enough for me in the past," he

said as he took a sip from his mug and smiled. "Just the way I like it, strong enough to take the paint off the side of a barn."

"It's got some punch to it; I'll say that much," I said as I took another, more cautious sip.

"You get used to it after a while," he said, and then he let out a loud breath as he eased down into one of the living room chairs nearby. "What a night."

"Did you catch the bad guy yet?" I asked him with a grin.

"Not even close," he admitted. "How about you?"

"Like I said before, we have some suspects and a few motives, but that's about it."

Jake shook his head. "Truth be told, that's better than I've done. All I've been doing is listening to rumors, gossip, and hearsay."

"Are you kidding? That's where you find all of the good stuff," I said. "What have you got so far?"

He almost answered, but then he stopped himself short and just smiled at me. "No way. You go first."

"And then you'll chime in?" I asked him, glancing at the clock. I was running on borrowed time, but if it meant getting closer to Chester Martin's killer, I was willing to go in late for a month.

"We'll see," he said with that cryptic grin of his.

"Okay, here's what Grace and I have managed to gather so far. As of right now, our main list of suspects includes Vince Dade; Maggie Hoff and her husband, Nathan; and Shelly Graham."

"Are you sure that you're not forgetting anybody?" he asked me as he watched me carefully.

"Well, George seems to think that Kevin Leeds had some kind of problem with Chester, but I haven't found anything out about that yet."

Jake shook his head. "I'm not talking about this Leeds character; I'm talking about the mayor himself."

So, he'd heard about the argument between the mayor and librarian himself. "George explained all that away."

"Maybe to your satisfaction," Jake said, "but I still need to speak with him."

"I don't have a problem with it, but the mayor might. You haven't known George Morris for very long, so let me bring you up to speed on His Honor. The man's got a temper like nobody's business, and it comes out from time to time, especially when someone questions him about something. He's not very politic sometimes."

"That's an interesting trait for a mayor to have, but I'll take my chances. My eyewitness told me that George and Chester had a rather heated disagreement this afternoon. She sounded positive that it nearly came to blows."

"Jake, you can't take *everything* that Zelda Marks says at face value. The woman has been jumping at shadows for years."

The interim chief of police studied me for a moment before he said softly, "I never said that Zelda was my witness, Suzanne."

"My mistake," I said. "She was, though, wasn't she?"

"No comment," Jake answered, but from the twinkle in his eye, I knew that I was dead on.

"Fair enough," I replied, satisfied that I was right. After all, who else could have witnessed the argument but the librarian's second in command?

"So, that's it? No one else had even the ghost of a

reason to want to see Chester dead?" Jake asked me.

"Not that I've been able to find out so far," I said as I took a longer sip of his coffee. Either I was building up some immunity to the stuff, or it was starting to grow on me. I wasn't sure which scenario I was hoping for.

"You said something about motives earlier," Jake said, and then he glanced at the clock. "That's going to have to wait, isn't it? You've got to get to work, don't you?"

"No worries. I can push it back a little bit," I said.

"Are you sure?"

"Positive. I've been making donuts so long now that I could just about do it in my sleep, not that I've ever tried. Okay, here's what we've got so far. Vince is supposed to have lost a great deal of money on a land deal with Chester ten years ago. Next up, we have some folks saying that our former head librarian was fooling around with local gal Maggie Hoff. He ended the affair pretty recently, so she could have a motive, but then again, so could her husband, Nathan. If Shelly found out what was going on, she could have done it herself."

Jake took all of that in. "Ten years is a long time to wait to get revenge," he said after a few moments of silence.

"Evidently something stirred up the old memories recently."

"Was it just the two of them involved in the land deal?" Jake asked.

"Well, Momma and Chief Martin were a part of it, too, but evidently Vince didn't hold anything against the two of them for dropping out."

"That's interesting," Jake said, and then he remained

silent for a time.

"You don't think my mother or her new husband had anything to do with what happened to Chester, do you?" I asked him.

"Not until I hear something more direct than that. Now, if Vince had been the victim, I might have had to look at them, but as things stand, as far as I'm concerned they're in the clear."

"Do you honestly think that Momma or the chief could have done something to the man's own brother?"

"I've seen it too many times before to discount it out of hand," Jake said, and as he did, I saw how the burdens he'd carried over the years had truly begun to wear him down. "Some of the things that I've seen can't ever be forgotten."

"Your job has been tough on you, hasn't it?" I asked with a softened voice.

"More than I care to admit, and most likely more than I'll ever know," he said with true sadness in his voice. After a few moments, Jake shook his head, as though he were clearing the cobwebs from his mind. "Now, you need to get to work, young lady."

"Okay," I said as I looked at the clock and realized that I couldn't push it any further and still make my donuts on time. "You're right. Will I see you later today?"

"I'll try to drop by the shop before you close at eleven, but I can't make any promises," he said.

"I understand."

"Suzanne, you'll call me if you hear anything else, won't you?" he asked me as I put the mug on the coffee table, stood, and then stretched.

"I promise," I said. "How about you?"

He just shook his head and laughed. "You need to change."

"Does that mean that you don't love me the way I am?" I asked him, intentionally misunderstanding him.

"Of course I do," he said as he stood and wrapped me up in his arms. It felt good, safe somehow, standing there, and I never wanted the moment to end, but after ten seconds, he broke free. "If you're going, you need to go right now."

"I could always call in sick," I said with a smile.

"I know you better than that. You wouldn't do that to Emma," he answered knowingly.

"You're right. Sometimes I hate that about you."

"It's just going to be a burden that I'll have to carry," he said with a smile.

"Can you stay up long enough for me to grab a quick shower and change my clothes?" I asked him.

"Take your time. I doubt I'll be able to sleep at all tonight," he said.

Four minutes later, I was back downstairs, but he'd taken my place on the couch, curled up with my blanket and snoring softly.

I left him with a kiss on the forehead, but he didn't even stir.

The poor man was exhausted, so I decided to let him get every second of sleep that he could manage before he had to hit the streets of April Springs in the morning searching for Chester Martin's killer.

"Good morning," I told Emma when she came into the shop an hour after I'd arrived. That was our schedule, and I was kind of partial to it. It gave me time to get the coffee started and work on the cake donuts by myself, but as the work picked up, as well as the dishes, it was nice having Emma there, too. She'd started out as just a dishwasher, but over the years she'd become a vital cog in my donutmaking machine.

"Hey, Suzanne. Can you believe what happened last night?"

"Are you talking about Chester Martin?"

"What else happened that could top that?" she asked me as she put on her apron.

"I can't imagine being murdered on the very day I was set to retire," I said.

"I don't want it to *ever* happen to me, but I know what you're saying. How's Jake managing?"

"You know him. He dove right into the thick of things," I said, purposely keeping my answers short and to the point. Emma and I had butted heads a few times in the past because of her father and her desire to please him. Sometimes that meant that Emma leaked information to him that I had, and it never worked out well for either one of us.

"Has he come up with anything yet?" she asked softly.

"No," I said. "I'm getting ready to drop donuts, so maybe we should drop this line of questioning, too, while we're at it."

"I'll be in the dining room," she said, quickly getting the hint. I wasn't really ready to start dropping batter into the oil just yet, but I didn't want to talk about Chester Martin's murder, especially not with Emma. After a few minutes, I had the first batter ready and loaded it into the heavy dropper. Swinging it back and forth to drive the batter to the exit point, I released the trigger and started dropping rounds of dough into the oil. I loved watching them cook, and after a few minutes, I flipped them expertly with the long wooden skewers I kept for just that purpose. Once they were ready, I pulled them from the fryer, placed them on the rack to drain for a minute, and then I iced them. Moving on to the next batch, I worked another twenty minutes before I was finished. Whether I was ready for it or not, it was time to bring Emma back into the kitchen.

When I opened the door to get her, she was waiting for me, tears in her eyes. "I'm so sorry, Suzanne. I shouldn't have asked you about the case. I don't know what I was thinking." The words tumbled out of her, and I could see that she was clearly upset by my earlier reaction to her probing questions. How could I stay mad at this young woman who meant so much to me?

I hugged her and patted her back gently for a moment. "Don't worry about it. It's fine."

"But it's not," Emma said when she pulled away. "Dad asked me to pump you for information. I should have said no, but sometimes it's hard."

"I'm sure that it is. Your father can be a very persuasive man at times."

Emma finally smiled a little. "It doesn't seem to work on your boyfriend, though, does it?"

I returned her smile with one of my own. "Jake has an infinite capacity to answer 'no comment' to just about any question a reporter asks him."

"Wow, you'd think it would be hard to do that."

"He doesn't seem to have any problem with it," I said. "Now, are you ready to hit those dishes?"

"You know me. I'm raring to go," she said.

"Liar," I replied, sticking my tongue out at her.

"No, I mean it. It's kind of therapeutic burying my arms up to my elbows in warm, sudsy water."

"Then by all means, let the healing begin," I said as I led her back into the kitchen.

Emma surveyed my cake donuts, all iced and ready to be placed on trays for our display, when she noticed something different. "Hey, that's new," she said as she pointed to my latest creation. "What is it?"

"I thought I'd try something different," I said. "Do you want to try a bite?"

"Sure," she said eagerly. "What exactly am I tasting?"

"You tell me," I said with a smile.

"Okay, I can do that," she said. Emma grabbed a knife and cut a small section from one of the donuts in question to taste. We'd both learned that there were only so many donuts we could eat in the course of a day before we got sick of them, and the additional pounds they brought with them, though I was a little miffed that my assistant's metabolism didn't seem to even notice the additional calories, whereas mine reveled in every ounce of the new poundage.

I watched her face as she took a bite, and to my relief, a smile blossomed. "Hey, that's really good. How did you do that?"

"I combined my hot chocolate recipe with the donut mix," I said. "Do you think the semisweet chocolate chips are too much? How about the chocolate glaze I made for them?"

Emma cut another bite and popped it into her mouth. "They're perfect just the way they are. If it were my decision, I wouldn't change a thing," she said.

"So, they're good enough to go on the menu?"

"You bet," Emma said. "What are you going to call them?"

"Triple Chocolate Treat sounds good to me. What do you think?"

"I was thinking more along the lines of just calling them what they are, Hot Chocolate Donuts, since that's the predominant flavor, but your name is probably better."

"Hang on, let me think about your suggestion," I said. "If we use your name, we can top them with a bit of marshmallow, too. The white dollop on top will really stand out, and it gives us a fun addition for cold weather. Yes, I like that a lot."

"How about Hot Chocolate Delights?" she asked. "That sounds perfect."

"Then make us a new sign, and we'll see how folks respond."

"You'd better be ready to add this one to the permanent winter lineup, because you've got a winner here."

"I hope you're right. You know how I love keeping my offerings fresh and fun."

"This should do the trick, then."

I was glad we'd worked through the situation we'd had earlier. I hated being edgy around Emma. She was so much more than a part of my work family.

During our break outside between making the cake donuts and letting the yeast donuts rise, I asked her, "How's your mother doing?" Sharon had helped me out in the past, along with Emma, running the donut shop whenever I was away, and when Jake and I finally went to Paris, I planned on having them run Donut

Hearts for a full week.

"She keeps asking me when you're going to take another trip," Emma said a smile.

"Is she trying to get rid of me?" I asked, laughing.

"No, but her travel budget is just about shot, and she's itching to take another trip. She says it's in her blood, now." Emma's mother financed her vacations with money she earned from helping run the shop while I was away, and though her husband didn't like to travel, Sharon's best friend enjoyed it as much as she did. It kept everyone happy, and I certainly wasn't about to judge them for it.

"I'll do my best to help her out as soon as I can," I said with a smile.

After our break, Emma and I got back into our routines, me making donuts while she fought valiantly to keep the dishes done right behind me. I'd been having her work the front more every week after we opened for business, something that she'd begun to warm up to lately. It gave me a nice respite at times, but generally, I loved interacting with all of the folks who came into Donut Hearts to enjoy a treat.

"Good morning. I'm so sorry for your loss," I said as I opened the doors to begin our retail day. Someone had been waiting for me, and I ushered Shelly Graham into Donut Hearts.

"Thank you," she said as she dabbed at her makeup. Shelly was a plump woman in her sixties, not hiding the streaks of gray in her hair, but embracing them. She wasn't a particularly handsome woman, but her bright smile was enough to make most folks not notice that. I'd liked her from the first time we'd met, but this was a different woman in front of me now. "Suzanne, can we talk?"

"Sure," I said as a few other folks started filing in. The folks who knew Shelly and, more specifically, her relationship with Chester began to offer their sympathies, a disrupting but sweet thing to have to deal with while trying to hold a conversation.

"Can we talk in private?" Shelly asked, clearly unhappy about the attention she was getting.

"Let's go back into the kitchen," I said as I led her around the counter and into the back.

Emma was listening to music on her iPod, but when she spotted us, she quickly pulled the buds from her ears. "What's up?"

"Do you mind covering the front?" I asked.

"I'm happy to do it," Emma said, pausing just long enough to smile sadly at Shelly. "Sorry about Chester. I always liked him."

"Thank you," Shelly said almost automatically in response. "So did I."

Emma nodded, and then she left us alone.

"Now, what can I do for you?" I asked her.

"Suzanne, I need your help," Shelly said.

"Absolutely. You know that I'll do whatever I can," I told her.

"Then find Chester's killer," she replied.

"Shelly, the police are already working on it around the clock."

"I've heard all about your boyfriend, but we both know there are things you can do that he can't. Are you trying to solve the murder, too?"

Even though that was exactly what I was doing, I

was reluctant to admit it. "What makes you ask me that?"

Shelly frowned. "Suzanne, I've listened to Phillip Martin over the past few months enough to realize that you're a pretty good investigator in your own right."

"What did he say about me?" I had to wonder what the chief said when he didn't think that it would ever get back to me.

"That despite his protests to the contrary, a lot of times he wasn't all that upset when you and your friend Grace got involved in his cases. Those were compliments given grudgingly, believe me. He respects what you bring to the table."

"I should thank him for saying that."

"I wouldn't do that if I were you," Shelly said. "I doubt that he'd even admit saying it. You know how men can be sometimes."

"As a matter of fact, I do," I said. She was right, too. I'd have to take the secondhand compliment and be satisfied with it.

"So, you'll look into it?" Shelly asked.

"I'll try, but honestly, I'm not sure what I can do that Jake isn't already doing."

Shelly took a step closer to me, and I could feel her breath on my face as she said, "Jake may know the law, but you know people. I'm begging you to help out."

"There's no need for that," I said quickly. In all honesty, her intensity was making me a little uncomfortable.

My response seemed to satisfy her. "Thanks. I can't tell you what a relief it is to hear you say that."

"Don't give me too much credit. I can't promise results, just that I'll do my best."

"It's all that anyone can ask of you."

There was something in her voice, a catch of concern that worried me a little. "Shelly, is there something that you're not telling me?"

"What do you mean?"

"You're holding something back, aren't you?" The furtive look downward confirmed my suspicion. Over the years, I'd grown pretty adept at reading people's body language, and Shelly was definitely trying to keep something from me. "What are you not telling me?"

She looked as though she were about to cry, but after a few moments, she gathered herself back up. "Suzanne, I don't like admitting this to anyone, but I'm afraid," she finally said in a near whisper.

"Afraid of what?"

"What else? That I might be next."

Chapter 7

Her answer completely caught me off guard. "What possible reason would the killer have to come after you?"

"How should I know? Maybe whoever murdered Chester thinks I know something."

"Do you?" I asked.

"I don't know. That's what is so frustrating," Shelly said, the tears coming unbidden now. "Why do you think that I'm so worried about it? I have half a mind to go back to the lodge, throw everyone out, send the staff home, lock all the doors, then hole up there until someone catches the murderer. Not that it would be that hard to empty the place this time of year. For the next four days, we might as well close down, since we don't have a single guest registered." She paused and then nodded. "You know, that's really not that bad an idea. I think that's exactly what I'm going to do."

"If it helps you feel safer, then you should," I said, "but I think your worries are unfounded."

"Do you really think so?" she asked me, as though she was daring to let a little hope into her heart.

"I do," I said, but I must not have sounded all that convincing.

"I hope you're right," she said, and then she took out a business card and jotted something down on the back of it. "This is the landline number to the lodge, since we don't get cell phone service up there. If you need anything, and I mean anything at all, or if there's a break in the case, don't hesitate to call me. Will you do that?"

"I promise," I said as I tucked the card into the front pocket of my jeans.

"Okay. Thank you."

As she started to go, I asked her, "Shelly, do you have one more second?"

"Sure, what do you need?"

There was no delicate way to ask her, so I decided to come right out and just do it. "Where were you when Chester was murdered?"

If she was offended by the question, she didn't show it. "As a matter of fact, I was on my way down the mountain for his party. One of my guests discovered when he was checking out that he'd lost a valuable set of cufflinks, and he accused one of my maids of stealing them."

"What happened?"

"I insisted that he check through his luggage again, with me watching him, and what do you know? They turned up after all."

"Was he trying to scam you into reimbursing him for them?" I asked.

"Either that, or he'd just overlooked them somehow the first time he checked. I like to think the best of the folks who come to stay at Storm Cloud, but sometimes it's hard to do. Anyway, I didn't make it down the mountain until Chester was already gone. You know what? I'll never forgive myself for not being there for him in the end. He asked me to come early, but I couldn't seem to get away."

"That might have worked out in your favor. Showing up early just might have put you in harm's way yourself," I said, relieved that she had a solid alibi. Well, it would be solid after Jake or I got confirmation from the accusatory guest. I'd learned over the years to confirm everything that a murder suspect told me, no matter how mundane it might be. Whether I liked it or not, people lied sometimes, and as hard as it was for me to accept, sometimes they even lied to me.

"Who knows? Maybe I could have prevented it if I'd been here," Shelly said, bringing me back into the moment.

"You'll drive yourself crazy thinking like that," I said. I'd wanted to ask her if she'd known about Chester's affair with Maggie Hoff, but if her alibi checked out, there would be no reason to mention it now. On the off chance that she hadn't known, I certainly didn't want to be the one who spoiled the memory of her late love for her.

"Yes, you're probably right. Still, it was a terrible thing, what happened to my Chester."

"Nobody's going to disagree with you there."

"I can think of one person who would."

"Who's that?" I asked her.

"Whoever killed him," she said sadly. After a moment, Shelly shook herself a little, as if trying to wipe away the memory of what had happened to her late boyfriend. "Thanks for taking the time to talk to me. After discussing it with you, I've made up my mind for sure. I'm leaving town as soon as I can get out of here."

"Be sure to talk to Jake Bishop before you go," I said before she could get away.

"Why should I do that?" Shelly asked. "There's nothing that I've told you that you can't share with him yourself."

"It doesn't work that way, Shelly," I explained.

"Jake is running the official police investigation, whereas Grace and I are just snooping around the edges."

"I get that, but why do I need to speak to him before I go?"

Did I really have to explain it to her? "Think about how it would look if you suddenly left town without explanation."

Shelly considered that possibility, and after a few moments, she said, "It would make me look as though I were guilty and running away from something."

"It just might," I said, though I was positive that's exactly what it would have done.

"Okay, I can do that. I'll find him first, and then I'll head back to my lodge," she said.

As she started for the door, I said, "I'll walk you out."

As we left the kitchen and walked back out front, I was surprised to see Jake standing at the counter speaking with Emma. "What do you know; you're just the man we were looking for," I said.

"Is that a good thing or a bad one?" Jake asked as he nodded toward Shelly.

"It's always good. Jake, have you met Shelly Graham?"

"We spoke briefly last night," he said, and then he turned to her. "Are you feeling any better? Is there any chance that we could have that chat sometime today?"

"We can do it right now, if you'd like," Shelly said, and then she looked around the donut shop at the sets of inquisitive stares pointing straight at her. "Only, can we do it outside?"

"Absolutely," Jake said. As he led her out the door, he turned back to me and added, "Don't go anywhere. I'll be back."

"There's nowhere else that I need to be," I said with a helpful smile.

He returned it briefly, and then told Shelly, "After you."

Once they were outside, I glanced at Emma, who was making it a point not to notice what had just happened. Well, if she wasn't going to comment on it, then neither was I. After a moment, she asked me, "Suzanne, should I stay up here, or should I get back to those dishes now?"

"You can dive back in, but I might need you to cover the front again this morning."

"All you have to do is call me," Emma said as she departed.

I tried to watch as Shelly and Jake spoke outside, but my pesky customers kept coming in and ordering things. I really didn't mind the business, but it put my surveillance skills to the test.

After a solid five minutes, Jake came back in alone, but he didn't have a smile for me when he did.

"Is everything okay?" I asked him.

"To be honest with you, I have no idea at this point. She's leaving town. Did she tell you that?"

"She might have mentioned it," I admitted, "but in my defense, I told her that she had to talk to you before she took off."

"Thanks for that much, anyway."

"Did she tell you her alibi?"

Jake nodded. "If it sticks, then she's in the clear.

That's a mighty big if, though."

"I wouldn't think a guest would be that hard to track down."

"Ordinarily no, but Shelly told me that he paid cash, and he filled out the registration as Joe Jones."

"Do you suspect that might not be his real name?" I asked him.

"It sounds pretty generic to me, but we'll see. Anyway, she's going to call me from the lodge with his contact information."

"Keep me posted. So, not that I'm complaining, but what brings you by the donut shop so early?" I asked him. "Did you miss me, or were you just having a donut craving? If you were, I've got a new one you're going to love."

"None for me; thanks anyway," Jake said, clearly distracted. "I just wanted to tell you that I might not be back for dinner tonight."

"Did you get a hot new lead?" I asked him.

"No comment," he said with a smile.

"Not even for me?"

"No comment," he repeated.

"I just have one more question," I asked him.

"Go ahead and ask, but we both already know what my answer is going to be."

"Do you think so?" Then I asked him softly, "Do you love me?"

"You bet I do," he replied with a big grin. "I'll comment on that all day long. See you later."

"Bye," I said.

After Jake was gone, I was glad that he was still in town, even if he *was* there trying to track down a killer.

It wasn't that I didn't trust Chief Martin and his deputies to do it, but Jake brought a whole new level of detection to the table, and if Grace and I could somehow contribute to the capture, so much the better.

"Good morning, you two. What brings you by Donut Hearts?" I asked as my ex-husband, Max, and his girlfriend, Emily Hargraves, walked into the shop. "Did you have a sudden yen for donuts?"

"Always," Emily said. "You go first, Max. I'm going to need a little time to figure out what I want today."

Max nodded and smiled at her as he said, "Take your time, Emily. I've got all day." I didn't know how he managed it; the man I'd once been married to was as handsome as ever. It may have been because he kept himself in shape or that he could thank his genes, but I suspected that the real reason may have been because of the woman he was with. Dating Emily had changed my ex in many ways, turning him into the man that I'd always hoped he'd be when the two of us had been married. It had taken me a while, but I was finally able to honestly say that I was happy that he'd finally found someone. It probably didn't hurt that I'd found someone myself in Jake.

As Emily studied my offerings in the glass display cases, Max turned to me. "How are things with you, Suzanne? Can you believe that somebody killed Chester Martin in the library? I didn't know him all that well, but he seemed like a good guy to me. The poor man didn't even get to enjoy one day of retirement."

"It just goes to show you that you can't ever take anything for granted," I said.

"Tell me about it," he said as he looked lovingly at Emily again. "It's hard to imagine that we both saw him yesterday morning, and now he's gone."

"Where did you happen to see him, at the library?" I asked, curious about what the man had been up to the day of his death.

"No, he was leaving Kevin Leeds's place over on Oakmont. Emily and I were out jogging, and we saw Chester scowling at Kevin as we ran past them."

"What was he upset about?" I asked.

"I'm not even sure that he was scowling myself," Emily chimed in. "Neither one of them said a word to us as we passed them. They just waved, and then we were gone. It all happened in a split second."

"The man was angry. I'm sure of it," Max said.

"I'm sure that you are, but Max, we both know that you have an overactive imagination, especially when you're not working. Am I wrong, Suzanne?" she asked me.

"I'm sure that I couldn't say one way or the other," I told her, refusing to be drawn into that particular discussion.

Emily laughed at my response. "Come on, be honest; you were married to the man. Back me up on this."

I joined her with a chuckle of my own. "Okay, it's true."

"There, see? I told you. Max, you need to a new role to play."

"Hey, I keep auditioning, but no one seems to want me," he said, clearly a little hurt to have to admit it, especially in front of me.

"If there aren't any roles for you, then stage another

play yourself. You know you love directing your troupe of senior citizens."

Max shrugged. "Maybe you're right. I'll start digging through scripts this afternoon."

"Excellent," she said as she touched his shoulder lightly and then she turned back to me. "Suzanne, I'll have a hot chocolate donut, please, and make it to go. I have to get to work soon. My buddies Cow, Spots, and Moose will be waiting for me." The three aforementioned friends were Emily's childhood stuffed animals. Instead of storing them away in an attic somewhere, Emily had displayed them prominently on a shelf above the register of her little shop. In fact, she loved them so much that she'd named the place after them.

"What are they dressed up as now?" I asked her. Emily loved to clothe her stuffed animals in all kinds of outfits, and folks in town loved seeing what she came up with.

"They're between costumes at the moment, but I've got a few ideas I'm toying with. Have I done pirate outfits yet? I'll have to check the photo album." Turning back to her donut choice, she asked me, "Suzanne, is there any way that you could add some sprinkles and some extra marshmallow to mine?"

"For you, why not?" I asked as I embellished her donut to her specifications. Emily was known for her love of toppings, so it didn't surprise me that she wanted something a little fancier.

"How about you?" I asked Max after I delivered Emily's donut to her.

"Just coffee," he said.

"No treats today?" I asked.

Max patted his stomach. "I have to stay at my ideal weight, just in case something comes up."

"Got it," I said. "How about you, Emily? Would you like something to drink?"

"Let me see. How about some chocolate milk?"

"Aren't you afraid of going into some kind of chocolate shock?" Max asked her.

"Dear, sweet, Max, there's no such thing as too much chocolate. Am I right, Suzanne?"

"I'm with you wholeheartedly on that one," I said as I finished filling their orders. After Max paid, I gave him his change and said, "Thanks for coming by."

"Thank you for the goodies," Emily said as the two of them left the shop hand in hand.

After they were gone, I started thinking about what Max had said. I knew that he loved to exaggerate, but I also understood that he was a student of human nature, and if he said that Chester had been unhappy with Kevin Leeds, then I was just as sure that it was true. The only question in my mind was *why?* As far as I knew, the two men didn't have any connection at all. So why did his name keep popping up in my murder investigation? It was definitely something that Grace and I were going to have to explore. Speaking of Grace, I needed to see if she could get off work early and help me do a little sleuthing. As a supervisor for a cosmetics company sales team, her schedule was pretty flexible most of the time. I just hoped this was one of those occasions.

During the next lull, I grabbed my cell phone and called her.

"Hey, Grace. What's your afternoon look like?"

"Well, the clouds are starting to build up, so I'm

thinking that it might rain."

"That's not what I meant. Could you help me do a little digging into Chester Martin's murder this afternoon?"

"As a matter of fact, I've already cleared my schedule," she said. "Should I be there at eleven?"

"That may be when we close, but I have to run the register report, make out the deposit, and help Emma clean the shop."

"So then, five after?" she asked with a laugh.

"If you want to pitch in and help, that would be fine."

After a brief pause, she said, "Eleven thirty it is, then."

I swore I could hear her laughing as she hung up on me.

Excellent.

Now I had a plan for my investigation, and a partner in crime to help me carry it out.

Honestly, what could possibly go wrong?

Chapter 8

"Which suspect should we speak with first?" Grace asked as we left the donut shop together toward the end of the morning just after closing. Emma had offered to take the deposit by the bank for me, and I'd readily agreed, so I was free to sleuth for the rest of the day.

"I think we should tackle the married couple," she said firmly.

"Really? I was actually kind of hoping that we'd interview them last."

"Why is that?" she asked as she looked at me quizzically.

"I don't know. The whole subject matter is kind of delicate, and we certainly can't bring it up while they're together. Why do you want to speak with them first?"

"I suppose it's the whole 'two birds with one stone' philosophy."

"If they're together, we're going to have to find a way to split them up. If we can somehow manage that, would you like to take Nathan or Maggie?" I asked her as we got into my Jeep and I started driving toward the Hoff house.

"Suzanne, we both know that you're better with the men," she said.

"I can't say that that's entirely true."

Grace grinned at me. "Okay then. Have it your way. You take Maggie."

I thought about questioning the woman about her affair with Chester, something that wasn't public knowledge as far as I knew, and how I could delicately

ask her for an alibi for the time of the murder. I
decided that maybe I'd be better off with Nathan after
all. "No, you're right. You take the cheating wife, and
I'll deal with the spurned husband."

"When you put it that way, I'm not sure that I like
that, either," Grace said.

"Well, we need to decide fast, because we're here."
My best friend looked surprised to see that we were
already at the Hoff house. "How did I miss that?"

"You were too busy trying to convince me to take
Nathan on, and April Springs isn't all that big a town,"
I said with a smile. "So, first off, we need a strategy to
divide and conquer these two."

"I could always tell Maggie that she won a cosmetics
kit from my company," Grace said.

"Do you happen to have one in that big purse you
always carry around with you?"

"You never know," Grace said with a grin as she
started rooting around in the voluminous bag. After
thirty seconds, she came up with a lipstick sampler and
a small zippered plastic bag containing several
different sample sizes of blush. "It might not be much,
but I'll sell it as something much bigger before I give it
to her."

"That I've got to see," I said.

"Then watch the master and learn," Grace said with
a smile as we approached the front door. "Have you
decided what you are going to tell Nathan?"

I thought about it for a second, and then I came up
with something that I thought was fairly good. "Well,
he came by the shop last month to buy some donuts for
his office. I'll tell him that we drew his business card
out of the fishbowl today, and that he's won a free

dozen donuts."

Grace frowned as her finger hovered over the doorbell. "You don't normally do giveaways, and I've *never* seen you collect business cards, in fishbowls or any other bowls, for that matter."

"You know that, and so do I, but what are the chances Nathan's going to remember what he did a month ago? Do you think he's going to challenge me and refuse the donuts? If he does, he'll be one of the first men I've ever known to be able to do it."

"Good point," she said. "So, if he won donuts, where are they? You don't even carry a purse, and if you did, you certainly couldn't jam a dozen donuts into it."

"I was never going to claim that I had them on me," I said with a smile. "Now, ring the doorbell and let's see what we get."

I was ready for one or the other of them, but when they answered the door together, I was a little flustered. Nathan was a former high school football player who had grown lazy over the intervening years, and he had the paunch to prove it. He must have been thirty pounds over his playing weight, and he didn't wear it very well. Maggie, on the other hand, had kept herself in great shape since high school. Though she was a good twenty years my senior, I would have killed to have that body. Her hair was flaming red, and it looked natural to me, though I was no expert in hair coloring. I wondered if she cultivated a temper to go along with her hair color, and I had a suspicion that I was about to find out.

"Hello," she said as she looked at us quizzically. "May we help you?"

I was at a loss how to respond when Grace spoke up. "As a matter of fact, we're here to help you. Today's your lucky day."

"Me?" she asked suspiciously.

"Yes, you."

"Both of you, actually," I interjected. "We've been doing a giveaway at the donut shop, and Nathan, you won a dozen donuts of your choice. Do you remember putting your card in the drawing last month?"

Maggie frowned at her husband. "You swore to me that you'd stopped sneaking treats. Is this how you keep your word to me?"

"Honestly, it was so long ago that I don't even remember entering." He turned to me and said, "I'm afraid you've made a mistake."

"You came into Donut Hearts last month," I said, sticking with my story, even though it was clearly getting him in trouble with his wife. "I'm sorry it took me so long to get back to you." Then I turned to Maggie as I added, "As my way of apologizing, my friend here is giving you a mini makeup kit as well. That way you both win today."

That got Maggie's attention. "Where's my prize? I don't care about the donuts, but I'll take whatever else you're giving away. We're both off work this week, but this genius I'm married to forgot to make our hotel reservations, so we're having a staycation. Have you ever heard anything so ridiculous in your life?"

"I don't know," I said, "Under the right circumstances, I think that it could be nice."

"See? That's what I said," Nathan responded.

"You say a lot, don't you?" Maggie asked acidly, and then she spotted the pouch in Grace's hand. "Is that all

I get?"

Before Grace could answer, Maggie snatched the case out of her hand and opened it. After peering inside, she frowned at my friend. "It's not much, is it?"

"Don't underestimate the value of my gift. Those samples are highly prized," Grace said.

"Okay, if you say so," Maggie said, and then she started to close the door.

"Hey, what about my donuts?" Nathan asked as he looked at me.

"Forget about them. You don't need them," his wife replied harshly, and then she slammed the door the rest of the way shut.

"What just happened here?" Grace asked me as we stood on the stoop alone. Both of us were clearly stunned by the recent turn of events.

"I believe that we just got dismissed," I said, "and neither one of us even got to ask a single question."

"Wow, that Maggie's a force of nature, isn't she?"

"You say that almost as though you admire it," I replied as we headed back to my Jeep.

"No, ma'am, not in the least. That was a real bust, wasn't it? Should we just give up and go home with our tails tucked between our legs?"

"No, we can't let one disaster stop us, even if it was with two of our suspects at the same time," I answered. "We need to press on now more than ever."

As we got into the Jeep and I started driving, Grace said, "Well, we should look on the bright side of things."

"I'd love to hear what your idea of a bright side is."

"It can't get any worse than this," she answered.

This time, though, it just so happened that she was

wrong.

Chapter 9

"So, should we speak with Vince Dade next or Kevin Leeds?" I asked.

"I picked the first two, and we both know what a disaster that session turned out to be," Grace said, "so I'm willing to let you choose this time."

"Fair enough," I said with a smile.

"You're not even going to try to make me feel better about what just happened, are you?" Grace asked me with a smile.

"No, ma'am, not on your life," I answered happily.

For some reason, that made her laugh, and all of the earlier tensions about our most recent failures left us. After a moment, I said, "Let's tackle Kevin Leeds. He comes into the donut shop every now and then, so at least we've got that much going for us."

"That's okay by me," Grace said as she glanced at her watch. "If we're lucky, he should be on his lunch hour right about now."

"How could you possibly know that?" I asked her as I slowed the Jeep.

"Keep driving. I called the bank and asked about him."

"And they just told you his work schedule over the phone without any kind of explanation?" I asked her.

"Hey, it's not as though it's a state secret or something. Head back to the park near the donut shop. Apparently he likes to brown bag his lunch on a bench near Donut Hearts. From what I've heard, he's the cheapest man on the planet. If it's free, he'll take it, no matter what it is."

"That's been my experience with him in the past, but I'm not sure how it helps us. Well, at least I know the way there," I said as I turned the Jeep around and headed back to where we'd been half an hour ago. "Just out of curiosity, why didn't we speak with Kevin first?"

"That's easy enough to answer. He wasn't on his lunch break then," she said.

"Fair enough. Is there anything else I should know about before we speak with him?"

"After we chat, I'm going to want to go to the Boxcar and grab a bite to eat. I'm getting kind of hungry myself."

"That sounds great," I said, happy for at least something to look forward to. Questioning suspects wasn't my favorite thing to do in the world, so a reward for doing it was always welcome. I knew that it was critical to our investigation to get as much information as possible from the folks we suspected, but they didn't have to tell us anything, a fact that I was only too aware of most of the time. That meant that sometimes Grace and I had to push harder than we would have liked just to spur reactions from our suspects, and that had left some bad feelings in the past from folks who had turned out to be innocent after all. I'm sure that it was just an occupational hazard of being a detective of any sort, but that didn't make it any easier when people started avoiding both me and my donut shop. If murders kept happening around me, sooner or later I might have to go all the way outside of April Springs in order to keep my customer base up.

"Sorry, but I don't have enough food to share with both of you." Those were the first words out of Kevin Leeds's mouth the moment he saw us approaching him. I already knew that the man was cheap, always hoping to buy day-old donuts from me instead of the fresh ones. He couldn't believe it when I'd first told him that we gave them away to the church for the less fortunate, but I had finally managed to convince him that I was telling the truth.

"That's okay. We're on our way to the Boxcar to have lunch," I said. "Mind if we join you on your bench for a few minutes before we go in?"

"That's fine with me. It's still a free country. At least it ought to be," he said. "I can't believe you two can afford to eat over there."

"Trish's prices aren't all that high," Grace told him.

"Maybe not for you, but they're high enough for me," he replied. From one look at his sandwich, it appeared to be mostly mustard between two slices of bread. The bologna was sliced so thin that I wasn't sure that he would even be able to taste it. "There's nothing wrong with saving a little money when you can."

"We couldn't agree with you more," I said, and I caught a glimpse of Grace as she looked skeptically at me. It was a funny face, and I wanted to laugh, but it would be too difficult to explain to Kevin. "It was terrible what happened to Chester Martin, wasn't it?"

"A real shame," Kevin said as he took a small, careful bite of his sandwich. I noticed that there was a baggie with some questionable-looking celery beside him, as well as an old soda bottle, filled now with water.

"Did you two know each other very well?" Grace asked him.

"No, not really," he replied. "We used to, but we hadn't hung out together for a long time."

"Funny, that's not what we heard," Grace answered. Kevin stopped taking a drink mid-sip and stared at her. "I'm sure that I don't know what you're talking about. What exactly did you hear?"

"That you two were fighting just before he died," she said.

"Somebody's been lying to you. I haven't been in a fight since the third grade," Kevin answered, and then he resumed drinking from his bottle.

"Not a fight, then, but more like an argument," I corrected.

"That's true enough, I suppose. Chester owed me ten dollars for the longest time, but he would never pay up. I heard a rumor that he was selling everything he owned and planned to move away from April Springs to start a new life, so I realized that my chances to collect my money were slipping away. When I went to the library looking for him, he wasn't there, so I went back home before my shift at the bank started. The next thing I knew the man was banging on my door demanding to see me."

"What was the ten-dollar loan for?" I asked, not sure that it was relevant to our investigation but curious about it nonetheless.

"That's hardly important now, is it?" Kevin said. "Now that he's gone, I'd just as soon not talk about it."

A man was dead, and all Kevin could think about was ten dollars the victim owed him? "If you don't mind, I'd still like to know."

"I repeat, why do you care so much about it?" he asked.

"Why wouldn't you tell us if it weren't important?" Grace asked from the other side. Kevin had to keep glancing from one side to the other as we spoke, something that was clearly making him uncomfortable.

"He borrowed it from me a few years ago. That's all that matters," Kevin said.

"And you were still fighting about it yesterday?" Grace asked. Neither one of us could believe that Kevin Leeds would let something like that go for a day, let alone a few years.

"As I said, I don't want care to discuss it."

"I just don't see what all of the fuss is about. Could ten dollars be all that important in the scheme of things?" I asked him.

Kevin shrugged as he reached into his coat pocket and pulled out a small notebook. He proudly opened a few pages, and I saw that the man had recorded every transaction he'd ever had, no matter how small, in his fine handwriting.

"Wow, I can't believe you keep such meticulous records," Grace said.

I was certain that she hadn't meant it as a compliment, but he took it as one anyway. "I know every penny I've ever spent since the first grade."

"And it's all in there?" I asked as I pointed to the tiny notebook.

"Of course not. This just contains my most recent income and my various expenditures." He closed the book and showed us both the paper cover. "I got these notebooks on clearance for next to nothing. They were the best investment I've made in years."

I was about to ask him something else when I heard a buzzer go off. Kevin put the last bite of sandwich in his mouth, followed it with a drink of water, and then folded his paper lunch bag neatly and tucked it into his pocket. "If you'll excuse me, I have precisely seven minutes in which to walk back to the bank."

"Mind if we tag along and walk with you?" I asked him. We hadn't come anywhere close to asking enough questions yet, and I didn't want to let him get away until we had.

"Sorry, but that's my private time reserved for personal reflection," Kevin said, and then he was gone.

Grace and I watched as he walked away, and then we turned to each other and shook our heads.

"Apparently we're not as good at investigating as we like to think we are," I said.

"Apparently," she replied, echoing the sentiment.

"What should we do about it?" I asked her.

"Well, when all else fails, we could always eat."

"Do we even deserve a meal after three bad interrogations in a row?"

"I'm not about to base my food intake on whether I deserve it or not," Grace replied. "Feel free to punish yourself if you'd like, but I'm starving."

"Well, I've never done well on an empty stomach," I replied.

"Then we'll tackle Vince Dade after we eat lunch."

"Okay. I give in," I said as we headed for the Boxcar.

"Funny, but you didn't fight me on that very hard."

"Did you want me to?" I asked her.

"No way. What are you going to have?"

I shrugged. "Maybe I'll take a chance on whatever

special Trish is running today. Whatever it is, I know that it's bound to be good. How about you?"

"I'm sticking with my tried and true: hamburger, fries, and sweet tea."

As soon as she said it, I realized that was probably what I should get as well. "We'll make it two, then."

"No, sorry, but you've already committed to the special," Grace said with a grin.

"How is that possible? We haven't even walked inside yet." It was true, though just barely. We were on the steps and one more foot from the front door.

"Okay, I'll let you slide this time," Grace said as she held the door open for me.

"No, you're right. I'm going with my first choice after all."

"Even if it's liver and onions?" Grace asked mischievously.

"Trish wouldn't do that to me," I said.

"We both know that some folks just love that meal."

"No doubt about it. I'm just not one of them." I was relieved to see the special was meatloaf, mashed potatoes, and green beans, one of my favorites.

"Hey, Trish," I said with a smile, knowing that I was going to love my lunch.

"Sorry, but you just missed him," Trish said as her ponytail bobbed once in the air.

"Who exactly did I miss?" I asked.

"Jake, of course," she answered, clearly confused. "Weren't you meeting him here?"

"Why? Did he say that I was?"

"My mistake," Trish said. "Grab any table you'd like and I'll be right with you."

I didn't budge, though. "Trish, what aren't you

telling me?"

"Nothing, not a thing, nothing at all," she said, but the diner owner didn't make eye contact with me, something that was a dead giveaway that something was going on.

"Trish," I repeated, this time much firmer.

Blurting it out as though it cost her money to say each word, my friend the diner owner said, "He was here with another woman, okay?"

Chapter 10

"Another woman? Are you sure?" I asked loudly, not caring if some of the folks already eating at the Boxcar had paused to listen to our conversation.

"She was a woman, all right. She might have been wearing a suit, but there was no hiding those curves," Trish said. "Sorry. I shouldn't have said anything."

"We all know that's not true, and I appreciate the heads up," I said as I reached for my cell phone and headed back out the door. Grace started to come with me when I stopped her. "Grab us a table and order. I'll take the special after all. I love meatloaf."

"What if you need to go somewhere to straighten this out after your telephone conversation?" she asked me.

"Don't worry. I'm sure that it's fine," I said.

Grace just shrugged, and then she and Trish shared a furtive glance that I was sure I wasn't supposed to have seen.

It just made things that much worse. The entire town knew that Max had cheated on me when we'd been married, so it was understandable that everybody might be worried that Jake might do the same thing, but I had a distinct advantage over them: I knew my boyfriend.

Jake answered on the second ring. "Bishop here," he said.

"Hey. I heard you had a pretty nice-looking lunch companion today," I said, allowing the smile to come out in my voice.

Jake laughed, a very good sign indeed. I trusted him

completely, but it was nice to know that he hadn't been caught doing something that I wouldn't approve of. "This town is something else, isn't it? Kelly and I left the diner three minutes ago. Did Trish call you?"

"Actually, Grace and I must have just missed you. We're at the diner right now," I said. "Are you talking about Kelly Blakemore?" I'd met Kelly twice, a fellow investigator Jake worked with. She was a lovely woman, there was no doubt about it, but she also happened to be devoted to her husband, a former linebacker for the Carolina Panthers professional football team. "What was Kelly doing in April Springs?"

"Take a guess. The Chief sent her to talk me out of retiring."

Actually, that was a pretty smart move on Jake's boss's part. There were few men alive who could say to no to Kelly if she put her mind to it. "What did you tell her?"

"I thanked her for caring enough to come, and then I apologized to her for the wasted trip. I meant what I said, Suzanne. No matter what happens next, that part of my life is over, once and for all."

"Are you sure about that?" I asked. "I'm a little worried that you might miss the excitement of your old job if you quit now."

"With you around, how is that even possible?" he asked with a chuckle. "Kelly just left, and I'm trying to track Vince Dade down. Any ideas where I might find him?"

"Honestly, we were going to look for him ourselves as soon as we ate."

There was a pause, and then Jake said, "Fine, just as

long as I get to him first. Have you spoken with any of
your other suspects yet?"

"We have, not that any of the conversations did us
any good." I told him the painful details of each
encounter, and to his credit, he was sympathetic to our
frustration.

"You know as well as I do that happens in
questioning more often than anyone likes to admit," he
said. "It's not nearly as easy as they make it look in
books and movies."

"It still doesn't make it any easier to accept, though,"
I said.

"Nor should it. Listen, I really do have to run. If
you find Vince first, go ahead and take a shot with him.
You never know. You might just get lucky."

"Goodness knows that I'm due a little. See you later.
I love you."

"And I love you right back," he said before he hung
up.

I tucked my phone back into my pocket and found
Trish and Grace both trying to look nonchalant as they
stared out the door at me. Putting on a fake frown, I
stomped up the steps toward them. After all, why
shouldn't I have a little fun with them before I told
them what had really happened?

"What did he say?" Grace asked softly as I
approached them.

"You're not going to believe this," I said, trying to
build up a little frustration in my voice so they
wouldn't know that I was just playacting.

"Suzanne, I'm sure that it was all harmless enough,"
Trish said hastily. "They're probably just old friends. I

need to learn to keep my mouth shut."

"Don't you dare apologize. You were just looking out for me," I said.

"What did he say?" Grace asked. "Is it over?"

I suddenly felt bad about teasing them. It was time to end this. "It was all perfectly innocent. I've known the woman for years. Jake works with her. Or should I say worked."

"Why was she here, then?" Grace asked.

"It turns out that her boss sent her to get Jake to reconsider his resignation," I explained. "It was all a perfectly understandable mistake."

"That's a relief," Trish said. "I still need to be a little more careful about what I say."

I hugged her lightly. "Don't ever stop caring enough about me to tell me the truth."

Trish looked surprised by the gesture. "The same goes for the two of you, you know."

"You don't have to worry about us," Grace said with a grin. "We're both honest to the point of brutality sometimes." Her smile faded as she turned back to me. "You didn't answer my question, though. Is he going back?"

"No, he sent her on her way," I said. "One thing that I've learned about Jake is that once he makes up his mind about something in his life, there's very little chance that he's going to change it again without a very good reason."

"So, are we happy about that?" Trish asked me.

"Actually, we're ecstatic," I said.

"What's he going to do for a living, though?"

"That's the beauty of it," I said. "He has no idea. One thing that he has repeatedly said that he won't do is take over the police chief's job, even though it's pretty clear that Chief Martin is finished with it himself."

"So, we'll be in need of a new police chief soon," Grace said. "Any chance that you might run for office, Suzanne?"

I looked at her in disbelief. Had my best friend lost her mind? "I wouldn't do it if you paid me a million dollars," I said. "Besides, I already have a job."

"Isn't it tempting to run, though?" Grace asked.

"Not even a little bit," I said. "Now let's eat. I'm starving."

"The only free table is right here beside me. I hope that's okay," Trish said.

"That sounds wonderful to me," I said.

When Grace agreed, we took our seats beside the register. Trish smiled at us as she offered menus. "Do you even need to look at these?" she asked.

"I'll have the meatloaf special," I said as I refused it.

"Make that two," Grace said, surprising me with her choice.

"I thought you were going to have a burger."

"Hey, a gal's entitled to change her mind, isn't she?"

"Are you kidding? I consider it my natural-born prerogative," Trish said.

I grinned at the diner's owner. "Two specials then, and two sweet teas."

"Coming right up."

As Trish ducked back into the kitchen, a large room formed from another boxcar that matched the one we were sitting in, Grace said, "I've got to admit that you had me going there for a minute."

"I'm sorry. I know that it was cruel. I just couldn't

help myself."

"Are you kidding? I applaud your inability to pass up a way to zing Trish and me. Just remember, though, payback can be brutal."

"I'll keep it in mind," I said. "By the way, Jake's on his way to speak with Vince Dade."

"I hope he has more luck than we've been having today," she said. "Have we ever had an investigation where we've been thwarted so much so soon?"

"Not even close, but we were probably due. What we really need to do is to get these folks away from their usual surroundings so we can isolate them a little. They're all just a little too comfortable as things stand right now."

"That sounds suspiciously like you've got a plan," Grace said.

"I wouldn't call it a plan quite yet. Right now it's more of an inkling."

"Those work, too. Care to share it with me?"

I shook my head. "Not just yet. I want to play with it a little more in my mind first before I say anything out loud."

"I totally get that," Grace said, and then she looked up as Trish brought us not only our drinks, but our food as well.

"That's the beauty of getting the special," Trish said as she slid the plates in front of us. "You never have to wait."

"This all looks delicious," I said as I took in the lovely sight of the diner food on my plate. The meatloaf was coated in brown gravy, and there was even a dollop of gravy crowning the mashed potatoes as well. One look at the green beans told me that they'd never seen the inside of a can, and I knew that they'd be delicious too.

"Trust me, it's tasty," she said with a smile. "I had mine before we started serving lunch."

The food was everything that I'd hoped it would be, and my appetite was satisfied by the time we paid the check and walked out into the crisp afternoon air. Cool weather was finally upon us, and it hadn't come a moment too soon as far as I was concerned. Folks tended to eat more donuts when the temperatures began to drop, but there were more reasons than that that made me love the cooler weather.

"Where to now?" Grace asked me as she buttoned her jacket slightly. My best friend favored the hot days of summer over every other time of year, so I knew that she was already in mourning over the fact that chilling temperatures were to come.

"Well, I hope that Jake has already spoken to Vince Dade, because he's the only name left on our list."

"What do we do if we can't speak with him? If Jake can't find him, what hope do we have?"

"We'll just have to figure that out if it happens."

Unfortunately, that's exactly what happened after all. All in all, it just wasn't our day.

It turned out that Vince Dade wasn't at his office or his home, either.

"Do you have any idea where else he could be?" I asked Grace as we left his workplace.

"The only other place I can think of is the bank," she said.

"Why would he be there?"

"Well, he's got his hands in a dozen different ventures, so he's got to get capital for it all somewhere. It's worth a try, isn't it?"

"I suppose it's as good a place as any to look," I said as I drove toward the bank.

It turned out that we didn't have to look for him after all.

When I glanced across the street, I saw the man himself coming out of the town hall.

Grace had been looking at the bank, so when I turned the Jeep in the opposite direction, she yelped a little. "Hey, what are you doing? The bank's over there."

"Maybe so, but Vince Dade is right here." I pointed to him just as he spotted us and turned to walk away in the other direction. "Come on. He's trying to get away."

"Vince, hang on a second," I called out as Grace and I hurried out of the parked Jeep.

"I don't want to talk to either one of you," he said as he kept walking.

"This will just take a second," I promised him, though I doubted that I could question him that quickly.

"That's what your boyfriend said. I didn't tell him anything, and I'm certainly not going to speak with the two of you. I just want to be left alone."

"I'm sure that you do, but wouldn't it be easier just to speak with us now and get it over with? If you do, we'll promise to leave you alone."

"Guess what?" Vince said as he stopped abruptly. "You're going to leave me alone anyway." There was nothing friendly or pleasant in the way he said it, and his statement sounded distinctly like a threat to me.

"What could it hurt to answer a few questions?" Grace asked.

"Go away," he said.

"Do you really think that it's going to be that easy to get rid of us?" Grace asked him, pushing the man a little harder than I would have dared to try.

He looked at her fiercely for a moment before he spoke again. "I'll just say this once. I'm not interested in being a part of your little investigation, and I expect you to respect my wishes on the subject."

There was a clear "or else" hanging in the air, but Grace started to follow him anyway as he stomped off. I put a restraining hand on her shoulder.

"Suzanne, we can't just let him get away."

"Grace, don't kid yourself. We never had him in the first place. You heard the man. He's not interested, and we can't exactly *make* him cooperate with us. If Jake didn't have any luck with him, there's no reason in the world to suspect that we would."

"I guess you're right," she said, so I removed my hand from her shoulder. "We've hit nothing but dead ends this entire day. Is there anything else we can do, or is this just going to all be hopeless?"

"I've got one idea," I said.

"Is it the one you were talking about before?" Grace asked me.

"No, that one is still percolating."

"Then what's the one that's already been fully brewed?"

"Let's see if Momma and the Chief will let us nose around Chester's apartment for clues," I said. "I was hoping that it wouldn't come to that, but right now, we're all out of other options."

"Do you think he'll let us?"

"If we ask him? Probably not. I don't plan on being the one to put it to him, though. I'm going straight to my mother."

"What makes you think that she'll be able to get his permission?" Grace asked. "Scratch that. The chief would walk through fire for her."

"Not only that, but Momma practically begged me to investigate Chester's murder. I can't see her refusing us permission to search his place, can you?"

"We won't know until we ask," she said.

I pulled out my phone and dialed my mother's number, and as I did, I found myself hoping that she'd agree and that Grace and I would be able to find something that might help us figure out who had murdered the librarian on the day before his retirement.

"Momma, it's Suzanne."

"You don't always have to identify yourself. I know my own daughter's voice, Suzanne."

Uh oh. She was in a bad mood; that much was clear from her tone of voice. "Maybe this isn't the best time to ask you for a favor."

"I'm sure that I don't know what you're talking about," she said. "What do you want?"

"We need to check out Chester's place. Could you ask your husband if it would be okay for us to look around?"

Momma surprised me by laughing when she heard the request, and I could hear a muffled conversation with her husband: "I told you that she'd ask."

Speaking to me again, she said, "The key is under the third flower pot on the left. Don't worry about disturbing anything. Jake has already had one of his deputies check the place out."

"It wasn't Stephen Grant by any chance, was it?" I asked, and I saw Grace's interest in the conversation perk up at the mention of her boyfriend's name.

"How should I know who he sent?" Momma asked, that mood back again.

"Thanks for the permission," I said, determined to get off the phone as soon as possible.

"Just find whoever did this," Momma said in a low voice. "Not knowing is making our lives absolutely miserable."

"Are you two having problems?" I asked her, and then I immediately regretted posing the question.

"Suzanne, you've been married before, so I shouldn't have to tell you that the first year is always the most difficult one. Good-bye."

I found myself holding a dead phone, so I slipped it back into my pocket.

"That went well, didn't it?" Grace asked me sarcastically.

"How could you tell?"

"I could hear your mother from all the way over here. Let me guess. Is there trouble in paradise?"

"No comment," I said, refusing to get into it with Grace. "All that matters is that we've got permission to search Chester's place, and we'd better go do it before either one of them changes their mind."

"I'm all for it," Grace said as we hurried back to my Jeep. "What do you think we'll find?"

"I don't know, but we can't do much worse than we

have so far, so it's not like there's much for us to lose."
Apparently my mother's mood was influencing my
behavior as well.

If Grace noticed, she didn't comment, which was one
of the things I loved about her. "That's the spirit!"

I just hoped that something would turn up.

If it didn't, I was going to have to refine my one last
idea, or give up our investigation before it really even
had a chance to get started.

Chapter 11

"I can't believe how small this place is," Grace said as she looked around. "It reminds me of the old joke about having to go outside to change your mind."

"It's modest, all right," I said, "but at least that should make it easy to search."

The key had been exactly where promised, and Grace and I had let ourselves into the late Chester Martin's humble little cabin. Nestled in a stand of cypress trees, the place had been hard to find at first. The rustic siding had been painted the exact same shade as the trees, and I had to wonder if that hadn't been Chester's intent all along. For a pretty social and outgoing guy, he was apparently a bit of a recluse in his private life.

"Suzanne, do you want the combination kitchen/dining/living room, or would you like the bedroom/bath/closet area?" Grace asked me.

"It's your call," I told her.

"If you don't mind, I think that I'll stay out here. Good luck. Should we meet back up in three minutes after we've tossed the place?"

"Let's at least try to be neat," I said. "After all, Momma and the Chief will be coming back soon enough to go through everything."

"That's true," my best friend said as she opened the first cabinet door she came to in the kitchen.

As she began to work, I headed back for the bedroom, wishing that one of us would find something that the police had missed.

I didn't have much hope for that happening, though.

I was nearly finished when I stumbled across something that was not exactly a clue — at least, I didn't think so at first. Then again, I didn't know what to think when I found it. Something had slipped under one of the drawers of a dresser jammed into Chester's closet, and it took me a full ten seconds to dig it out from beneath the wide array of hanging costumes the man owned. I was tempted to take a photo of Chester's outfit selection and send it to Emily. I thought she'd done a thorough job of outfitting Cow, Spots, and Moose in the past, but Chester could have taught her a thing or two about costume creation and design. It was clear from the fancy sewing machine, as well as the yards of unused fabric and myriad spools of thread, that the librarian had enjoyed making his own outfits, but none of that had attracted me.

I'd found a postcard, and what was on it left me more baffled than I'd been before I'd found it.

The full-color photograph on one side of the card sported a dense campfire filled with heavy flames, an odd enough image to send someone else, but on the reverse side, in the small space reserved for a message beside Chester's name and address, were three words written in bold block letters that matched the address: STOP OR BURN.

I was staring at the message trying to figure out what it might mean, so I didn't even hear Grace come in. It startled me when she asked, "That's kind of an odd message to send through the mail, isn't it?"

"I was just thinking the same thing," I said as I studied the card a little closer. It had a Forever stamp on it instead of a standard postcard stamp, so that wouldn't help us figure anything out about how old it might be. There was a cancellation stamp over it, but the ink was too faded to easily read.

"What's the date it was sent?" Grace asked as she took a closer look for herself.

"That's what I'm trying to figure out," I said as I headed back to the closet. I'd seen a deerstalker hat hanging on a pegged board with several other unlikely pieces of headwear, but this one had been different. Hanging from its peg was a monocle as well, and when I retrieved it, I saw that it was a magnifying glass. "This might help," I said as I held the magnifier up to the cancellation mark. It was a little clearer now, and I could actually make out the date a little better.

"When was it sent?" Grace asked eagerly.

"Three days ago," I said as I reached for my phone.

"Who are you calling?"

"Jake needs to see this," I said. "Any objections?"

"No, not a one," Grace said quickly, which was a good thing, because I wasn't about to change my course of action. It was one thing withholding information from Chief Martin, but I was not about to do it with Jake.

I got him on the fifth ring, just before I'd been about to hang up.

"Hey, Suzanne," he said hurriedly, and I knew that I'd caught him at a bad time. "Is it urgent?"

"No, it can wait," I said. "Are you okay?"

"Fine, just busy right now. Talk to you later."

He hung up, and I returned the monocle to the peg where I'd found it earlier.

"Is he too busy to talk to you, Suzanne?"

"Apparently," I said as I took a sheet of paper from one of the empty notebooks and folded it in half. Placing the postcard inside the fold, I held onto it, not that there would likely be any viable fingerprints still on it. Still, I hoped that Jake would appreciate the effort. "Did you have any luck searching your part of the cabin?"

"Not really. After looking through his things, I can tell you that Chester Martin was a man of simple tastes. I found twelve cans of chicken noodle soup in his pantry and three jars of peanut butter. Add those to the three loaves of bread he stored in his freezer, and I'm betting we know what the man ate every lunch and dinner that he was here."

"What did he have for breakfast?" I asked half in jest.

"I'm glad you asked," Grace answered with a smile. "There were three cartons of power bars and eight cans of pear halves in natural juices."

"Well, we've got his dietary habits covered," I answered. "Anything else?"

"No, I came up empty. What did you discover besides that postcard?"

I showed her the variety of costumes hanging in the closet, as well as the sewing machine. "Apparently, Chester was a man of many talents," I said. "I'm pretty sure that he made all of his costumes himself."

"Okay, but none of that information is all that useful, is it?"

"No, this search has been pretty much a wash. In fact, we could say that about the entire day, couldn't we? I've got a feeling that no one's going to cooperate with our investigation unless we do something drastic to shift the balance more in our favor."

"You know me; I'm all for dramatic acts. Are you ever going to tell me what you have in mind? Talking out loud about it might help clarify your thoughts."

"Why not?" I asked. "It's clear that it's our last hope of doing any good at all with this murder investigation."

As I drove Grace back home, I told her all about the plan that had been brewing in my mind. I wasn't sure if it was reassuring or not, but she was extremely enthusiastic about trying it out after I explained it all to her. I wasn't quite so willing to jump on board myself yet, though. First, I needed to talk it over with Jake and get his blessing.

After all, if my plan worked, it would drastically alter the course of his investigation as well as ours.

Chapter 12

"Hey, stranger. Are we eating together, or should I go ahead without you?" I asked Jake after I dialed his number from the front porch of my cottage. The place had been empty when I'd arrived, but it really hadn't come as that big a surprise, given my boyfriend's work ethic.

"If you can hold out that long, I can be there in half an hour," he said.

"I'm not trying to guilt you into coming back here," I said in a soothing manner. "I know how you get when you're working on an investigation."

"Right back at you," he said, and I swore that I could hear the smile in his voice.

"I'm not denying it," I said, adding the hint of a laugh. "How's it going on your end?"

"The truth is that no one in this town has any desire to tell me anything," Jake said flatly. "Frankly, I expected to get a little more cooperation than I'm getting right now."

"Have you considered the possibility that no one's talking to you because they know you're not a state police inspector anymore?"

"How could they possibly know that?"

"Jake, you weren't trying to keep your voice down when you told me. Someone could have picked it up without you even realizing it."

"Maybe, but I'm still a law enforcement officer," he said. It sounded as though he was a little hurt by the lack of intimidation his new office held.

"Of course you are," I said.

"How did Phillip Martin ever manage to do it? I'll be honest with you. His job is tougher than it looks."

"You should tell him that sometime," I said.

"Maybe," Jake replied in a tone that told me that he might admit it to me, but that was as far as he'd ever be willing to go.

"If you have the time, why don't you come back here, eat a little, and then you can regroup."

"The first part sounds good, but I have no idea what I'm going to do next."

"I actually have a thought that might interest you," I offered timidly.

"Go on, I'm listening. Don't keep me in suspense."

"I'd rather talk to you about it face to face," I answered.

"Fine. I'll see you soon, then."

"I can't wait."

After we hung up, I started digging through the cupboards, the fridge, and the freezer to see what I could make us to eat. I ended up going with omelets because they were easy and fast and I knew that Jake liked them as much as I did. The best part was that I could wait to start cooking them until he showed up. In the meantime, I chopped up a green pepper, a little ham, part of a leftover onion, and a few bites of turkey we had left over from an earlier meal. After that, I grated some cheddar and mozzarella cheese, and then I tucked everything back into the fridge.

As I closed the refrigerator door, my cell phone rang. Was Jake canceling on me already?

"Hey, Suzanne. It's Shelly Graham."

"Hi, Shelly. I was just talking about you not half an hour ago."

"That's why my ears must have been burning, then," she said lightly. "I just wanted to touch base with you and tell you that I'm back at the lodge. I never realized how isolated this place was with no guests or staff. I mean, I come up sometimes in the winter to check on things during our off season, but it's just weird being here alone this time of year."

"How would you feel about having some company?"

"Are you and Jake coming up? That would be great. I'll give you my best room, the honeymoon suite, not that I'm trying to put ideas into anyone's head. I—"

"I appreciate the offer, but that's not what I'm talking about. Shelly, what would you think if we brought our suspects with us there?"

After I explained the plan, she readily agreed.

"How are you going to get them all to show up?"

"I haven't quite figured that part of the plan out yet, but I'll come up with something."

Shelly hesitated for a moment, and then she finally said, "If you can manage it, it sounds perfect. Let them try to weasel out of what they did up here. I'll start getting the rooms ready the second that we hang up."

"Hold on. I have to get Jake to approve of my plan first."

"Suzanne, from what I've heard, you shouldn't have any problem convincing him that this is a good idea," Shelly said.

"I wish I had your faith in me. Like I said, don't do anything yet on my account."

"Okay. Out of curiosity, how many rooms do you think you will be needing?"

I counted the suspects in my head, making

allowances for the fact that Maggie and Nathan would most likely be sharing a room. Or not. "I'd say five max."

"That's just fine, because I've got ten rooms we can use. When will you know for sure?"

That's when I heard the front door open.

"Hang on one second." I put the phone to my chest as I called out, "Jake, is that you?"

"It had better be," he said as he came into the kitchen. "What's for dinner?"

"One second," I told him, and then I pulled the phone back to my mouth. "Listen, I've got to go. I'll call you back later when I know more," I said, and then I hung up.

"Who was that?" Jake asked curiously.

I ignored both of the questions he'd recently asked and wrapped my hands around his neck. Pulling him in for a kiss, I waited until it was over before I said, "I'm fine; thanks for asking. How are you?"

"Well, I'm better now," he said, and then he moved in for another kiss.

"I thought you were hungry," I said as I playfully pushed him away. Both of us were in infinitely better moods now. Why wouldn't we be? After all, we were together again.

"I am," he said as he sniffed the air. "I don't smell anything cooking. Aren't we eating here?"

"We are," I said as I turned a burner on and put the skillet on it. After it heated up, I dropped some butter in the center and watched as it sizzled.

"What can I do to help?" he asked.

"I've got it covered. Why don't you go wash up? We'll be eating soon."

"Glad to," he said.

I cracked five eggs into a bowl, added a splash of milk, and then I whisked them a little with a fork until they were mixed together. After that, it was just a matter of adding them to the hot butter in the pan. As the egg mixture began to set, I got out my filling, and five minutes later, we were ready to eat.

I just hoped that Jake went for my plan.

If he didn't, I wasn't at all sure what either one of us was going to do about furthering our investigations.

"What's this?" Jake asked as he walked into the dining room a minute later. He had the postcard I'd found in his hand.

"I found it at Chester's place," I said. Jake started to speak, but before he could, I added, "It was stuck under a drawer, and it was nearly impossible to find. I called you about it, but you were busy, remember?"

"That's good that you found it," he said a little too evenly for my taste. "I'm going to have to have a talk with the officer who searched Chester's place."

"It wasn't Stephen Grant, was it?"

One eyebrow shot up. "No, it was the new man, Blake. Why do you ask?"

"No reason," I said, glad that we hadn't gotten Grace's new boyfriend in trouble with his new, if temporary, boss.

Jake held it carefully by two edges as he asked, "Any idea what it means?"

"I haven't a clue," I admitted.

Jake set it back down carefully as he replied, "Neither do I. Well, I'm here now. Let's hear all about your plan."

"Shouldn't we eat first?" I asked as I cut the omelet into two portions and slid the larger one onto Jake's plate.

"Hey, I got more food than you did," he said.

"You're seriously not complaining about that, are you?"

"No. Not one bit. Forget I even mentioned it," he said with a slight grin. "Now talk."

I took a deep breath, and then I started to tell him my idea. "I've been thinking that the only way we're going to have any luck interrogating our suspects is to isolate them somewhere out of the way where we can be certain that we have their undivided attention."

Jake took a bite of his omelet, smiled, and then waved his empty fork at me. "Believe me, I'd lock them all up if I could, but there are procedures that I have to follow."

"How about if they isolated themselves voluntarily?" I asked as I took a bite myself. It was delicious, and I had to wonder how much of that had to do with the fact that I was starving. Trish's meatloaf had only held me for so long.

Jake put his fork down. "How are you going to get any of them to agree to doing that?"

"I'm still working out all the details. First I wanted to see what you thought of the general idea. I've already spoken with Shelly, and she's on board, and so is Grace."

"Who else have you told about this plan of yours?" he asked me a little warily.

"That's it; I promise."

"Let me think about this for a minute," Jake said, and then he went back to his omelet, though I noticed that he was eating much less heartily now. We continued to eat in silence, since I knew that anything I could add at this point could be detrimental in Jake's decision.

After he finished eating, he pushed his plate away. "That was amazing. You should seriously think about making food for customers for a living."

I smiled at him. "What a coincidence. I already do."

After another moment or two spent deep in thought, Jake looked at me before he spoke again. "There a few things we need to get out of the way up front before I agree to anything."

"I'm listening."

"First off, I can't be the one who invites anyone anywhere. In fact, there can't even be the whisper of an official investigation being conducted here. Is that understood?"

"Completely," I said.

"That means that you have to coordinate everything, including issuing the invitations and making the room assignments. Is that going to be a problem?"

"I'm ready to handle everything," I said. "You're at least coming too, aren't you?"

"Suzanne, you couldn't keep me away even if you tried locking me up. Exactly who are you going to invite?"

I ran through my list of suspects, and then I asked him, "Is there anyone I'm missing that you'd like me to invite, too?"

"As far as suspects are concerned? No, I think you've got that covered."

"Okay then, is there anyone who's *not* a suspect that I should add to my list?" I asked, curious about what Jake was thinking.

"Well, obviously you need to call Chief Martin and tell him what you're planning. If I know him, he's going to want to come, too."

"Don't worry about him. I can get Momma to keep him at home," I said as we started gathering our empty plates and glasses to carry into the kitchen.

"Hang on. That's not what I meant. As a matter of fact, it might be good having him there as backup."

"If he comes, we both know that Momma's going to want to come as well," I said.

"Is that a problem?"

"To tell you the truth, I'm not all that thrilled with the idea of putting my mother in harm's way," I said as I piled the dishes into the sink for later.

"I've got a hunch that you're not going to have a say in the matter," Jake replied. "I know you might not like including them, but the man's brother was killed on his watch. I can't refuse the chief's request if he wants to be at that lodge to help catch the killer."

"Nor should you," I said. "I don't know why I'm so worried. Momma and I can take care of ourselves."

"How well I know that to be true," Jake said. "Who else needs to know what we're up to?"

"Well, I don't see any way around the fact that you've got to tell your boss," I said.

"I'm not calling him, so forget it. I quit, and that's the end of it. He's no longer my boss, so I don't have to run anything past him ever again." Jake's jaw was set in a way that told me this topic was not up for discussion.

"I wasn't talking about your old boss," I said quickly. "I meant that you needed to tell George Morris. The mayor has a right to know what's going on."

"I'm guessing that he's going to want to come along, too," Jake said. "Not that I mind. He might be your mayor, but he's still got a cop's instincts from his years on the force, and those are in short supply around here sometimes."

"Let me ask you something, Jake. If you three — the current interim police chief, the most recent previous police chief, and the current mayor — are all out of town, who does that leave in April Springs to be in charge?"

"Stephen Grant's up for the job," he said without a moment of hesitation. "This will give him some good field experience in command. The kid's smart as a whip, and someday, he's going to make a fine chief himself."

"Is he ready for that much responsibility now, though?" I asked.

"Hey, I thought you were the man's number one fan," Jake accused me teasingly.

"That's not true. I'm second, next to Grace, but yes, I like him a lot. You didn't answer my question, though."

"I wouldn't ask him to do it if I didn't think he was ready for it," he said. "Besides, we may be getting ahead of ourselves."

"How so?"

"We don't even know if our suspects are going to bite on whatever story you're going to try to feed them yet."

I smiled at him. "Come on. I'm giving them all a free three-day weekend at a mountain resort. Do you honestly think that anyone is going to turn the offer down?"

"As a matter of fact, I do," Jake said.

"Hmm," I said after a few moments. "I could always just tell them that they won their trips."

"What contest did they each supposedly enter that they've won?" Jake asked. "I imagine they'll want to know, so you'd better have a sound answer for them."

I frowned for a moment, and then I answered, "Well, if you're going to be all logical about it, I'm not sure that I have a suitable answer."

Jake grinned broadly at me. "Think harder then, Suzanne."

"We could always say that we're having a special memorial service for Chester up there," I offered after a few moments of thought.

"The problem with that is that each one of these folks was fighting with Chester just before he died. It's going to be hard to get any of them to drop everything and take a trip to the mountains to celebrate someone they were unhappy with in the first place."

"Okay. Give me another minute. I'm not going to give up until I've got something."

"Take all of the time that you need. Do we happen to have any pie? I thought I saw some in the fridge the other day."

"Momma just brought over an apple-crumb-top pie. Help yourself."

"Don't mind if I do," he said. "Would you like a slice?"

"Why not?" I said, and then I started pondering different ways I could get my suspects to come. I must have weighed half a dozen ideas as I sat there, but they all sounded too transparent even to me to say out loud.

And then it hit me.

"How about if we just come right out and tell them that if they want to clear their names as suspects as soon as possible, they'll come to the lodge, but if they want to remain suspects in everyone's minds, then they can just stay home."

"So, now you're threatening them to get their cooperation?" Jake asked me.

I considered how that sounded, and then I nodded. "That just about sums it up. What do you think? Will it work?"

"There's only one way to find out," he answered with a slight smile. "Start calling them."

As I dialed the first telephone number, things suddenly got very real for me. I'd come up with this idea on a lark, but now we were actually going to go through with it. While I realized that it should be helpful isolating everyone at the lodge, it also might mean that the killer would be even more dangerous cut away from the rest of society. I prayed that I wasn't making a mistake, but it was too late to turn back now.

I only hoped that we were doing the right thing, and that no one else would die while we were in seclusion.

I wasn't sure that my conscience could take it.

Chapter 13

To my delight, by the time I had finished making all of the phone calls, only one of our suspects had declined the free trip and the chance to clear their name.

"Suzanne, I can't believe that you actually did it," Jake said as he watched me hang up on the last caller.

"It wasn't a complete success. I couldn't get Vince Dade to agree," I said, upset with myself for letting one of our suspects turn me down.

"Don't be too hard on yourself. You did better than either one of us had any right to expect," Jake said.

"But can we even do this without Vince, Jake?"

"Give him the night to think about it, and then ask him again in the morning. I suppose you might as well call our other guests who *aren't* suspects and invite them to the party, as well."

"At least I'm betting that I won't have to twist any of their arms to get any of them to come," I said.

"You're right about that. I've got a hunch that everyone is going to want to be there. We all need to be doubly careful while we're at the lodge. You know that, don't you?"

"Jake, I'm not about to take any foolish chances, especially when so many innocent lives are at risk."

He hugged me gently. "I know you won't. Go on and make your calls. At least this should be a happier batch for you to make."

"What are you going to be doing while I call everyone?"

He leaned back and looked a little pensive before he

spoke. "I'm going to try to figure out how to trap the killer and keep the rest of us alive in the process. How does that sound to you?"

"Like it's the best use of your time and resources," I said.

As we'd predicted, every one of our friends said yes immediately to our offer, and soon enough, we had a full house heading to the lodge the next day. After I finished making my calls, I looked around and finally found Jake sitting out on the front porch, despite the chill in the air after the sun had set. I put a spare blanket over his shoulders, which he gratefully accepted.

"Did you reach everybody we talked about?" he asked me.

"Everyone said yes," I said as I sat down beside him.

"Good. There's just one more thing. Did you happen to call Emma and Sharon and ask them to sub for you over the next few days at the donut shop while you're going to be in the mountains?"

In my haste to arrange the getaway for our guests and our suspects, I'd forgotten all about calling the mother/daughter team to see if they could take over for me for a few days. It was getting to be a habit with me, and I hoped that I hadn't been asking them too much, since I'd hate for the duo to say no. "I'll call them right now."

"Go right ahead and make that last call. I'm not going anywhere," Jake replied as he pulled the warmth in closer.

To my delight, Emma agreed the moment I asked.

"My mother will be absolutely delighted. Any special instructions for us while you are gone?"

"Just keep making the donuts and selling them, and we should be fine," I said. "Thanks again for doing this, and thank your mother, too."

"Are you kidding? We should be the ones thanking you. This will give us both a chance to work on our nest eggs. See you when you get back. And don't forget to be careful."

"Thanks," I said.

"That was a relief. They were happy to do it," I said as I rejoined Jake.

"One of these days, they're going to make you obsolete in your own operation; you know that, don't you?" he asked.

"Kind of like what you just did to yourself with the state police?" I asked with a grin.

"Touché." Jake took in a deep breath, and then he let it out slowly before he spoke again. "Suzanne, you're not in any hurry to retire from the donut shop, are you?"

I laughed at the very thought of it. "Not a chance. Just how old do you think I am?"

"I wasn't trying to insult you. After all, people retire at all ages," he said.

"Well, I'm not anywhere near ready to hang up my apron for good. Jake, we both know that you'd go crazy if you didn't have some way to fill your days yourself. It's way too early for you to even think about retiring for good."

"I know. I'm just not sure what it is that I want to do with the rest of my life."

I patted his shoulder. "Don't worry. You've got plenty of time to decide. In the meantime, let's see if we can figure out how to catch this killer."

The two of us batted around half a dozen ideas for the next hour before it was time for bed, but in the end, we weren't able to come up with anything that might even remotely work. In the end, we called it a night and decided to sleep on it.

After all, tomorrow was going to come earlier than either one of us was ready for.

"So, we've got an hour to kill on our drive up into the mountains," I said as Jake, Grace, and I headed to Shelly's lodge in my Jeep. "Should we try to come up with some kind of plan for when we get there?"

"I'm not worried about when *we* show up," Grace said from the seat beside me. "It's when our suspects convene that has me concerned. How about you, Jake?"

I glanced at my boyfriend in the rearview mirror. He'd readily agreed to climb in back, and I'd wondered why he hadn't opted to join me up front. Was there a reason for his isolation, or had he just done it out of politeness to Grace? Either way, I was curious to find out if he had any thoughts. "We might not have to have a grand plan after all."

"What do you mean?" I asked.

"Suzanne, we're getting all of these suspects together in an isolated place. That might just be enough to do the trick all by itself. It won't take much to stir the pot. As a matter of fact, I can think of a few ways to get the party started, but after that, I think we should all just step back and see what develops."

"To be honest with you, that kind of surprises me, Jake. You don't strike me as a particularly passive kind of guy," Grace asked him.

"In ordinary circumstances, I'm not," he said.

"But this situation is anything but ordinary, isn't it?" I asked.

"Exactly," Jake said as he nodded his approval. "I'm curious now, Suzanne. If our roles were reversed, what would you do to get the action moving forward if it were just the two of you doing this without my help?"

I considered it, and after nearly a minute, I said, "Well, I'd probably start by separating them."

"And how might you accomplish that?" he asked. I looked over to see Grace listening to our conversation carefully.

After a moment's thought, I said, "I'd most likely gather them all together in the main room, and then I'd call them one by one into another, smaller space."

"And just what would you do once you had them there?" Grace asked, clearly too curious to stay on the sidelines of the conversation.

"It doesn't really matter at that point," I said.

"What do you mean by that?"

"Grace, the implication of what the one not in the room with the rest of them is saying is really all that counts. When one person is speaking with me, the others are going to let their imaginations supply the crux of the conversation. Sure, I'd ask some pointed questions, but they wouldn't cover any ground that we all haven't already touched upon."

Grace turned back to Jake. "Would that work?"

"It just might," he said.

"Only you should be the one asking the questions, not me," I told Jake as I glanced back in the rearview mirror.

"Why not you?" he asked softly.

"Because this is one of those cases where the aura of authority is the only way that it will work. If I question them, no one has to take the ramifications of the outcome as seriously, but if you do it, it's bound to attract more attention. Do you disagree with that assessment?"

I glanced back again as I asked the question, and I saw the hint of a smile flee from his lips. "No, that makes sense. Is that what you'd recommend we do?"

"It sure is, but I didn't think you could get involved."

"I said that I couldn't play any part in getting them there, but if everybody is already assembled at the lodge, then I'm just interviewing suspects at that point," he said with a shrug. "Everyone except Vince Dade will be in attendance, and what is the investigating officer supposed to do when nearly every suspect he has — bar one — has decided to leave town together?"

"He doesn't have much choice but to follow them," Grace said with a grin. "That's pretty cool how you worked that out."

"Don't give me too much credit," he said. "This was all Suzanne's idea. I'm just trying to use the new scenario to my own benefit."

"And it sounds as though you've formulated a plan already," I said. "And here we have another forty minutes on our drive. What should we talk about now?"

"I'm not ready to stop planning," Jake said. "We might need to set more than one trap while we're here. By the way, did you call Vince Dade again yet?"

Blast it all, I'd forgotten all about approaching the one suspect who had refused the trip. "No. If you two can be quiet, I'll do it right now."

Grace got out her cell phone, dialed a number, and then held it up so I could talk.

Vince picked up on the first ring.

"Vince, this is Suzanne Hart," I said.

Before I could continue, he broke in. "If this is Suzanne, then why are you calling on Grace Gauge's phone?"

Sometimes I hated caller ID, though to be fair, there were other times that I absolutely loved it. "I'm driving, so she made the call for me. I was just wondering if you'd changed your mind about coming to the lodge."

There was a slight pause, and then Vince said, "I'm still not thrilled with the idea, but yeah, I'm coming. It's the only way I can think of to keep my name from being dragged through the mud. Is your boyfriend going to be there?" he asked after a slight pause.

I was about to tell him that Jake was with me even as we spoke when I felt a nudge coming from behind. I looked into the mirror and saw Jake put a finger to his lips as he shook his head. Did that mean lie to Vince? What good would that do? He'd see Jake soon enough. Instead of answering, I decided to ad lib a little. "I'm in the mountains, and this call isn't very clear. Vince, can you hear me? You're breaking up. I'll see you at the —
"

Grace chose that moment to hang up. "Why didn't

you let me finish?"

"Suzanne, nobody hangs up on themselves. It's more convincing that you were having reception trouble this way."

"I get it, but that doesn't mean that I have to like it."

I glanced back at Jake. "Why did you shush me just then?"

"I didn't want him to know that I was in the Jeep with you," Jake explained.

"But you don't mind him knowing that you are going to be there, too?"

"Of course not. Why should I try to hide that fact, when he'll learn about my presence there soon enough?"

"That's exactly what I was wondering," I said. "That begs the question as to why you didn't want him to know that you were in the Jeep with us."

"I was hoping that he might let his guard down and something would slip out," Jake admitted.

"Well, that was certainly all in vain," Grace said.

"You never know unless you try," Jake replied with a shrug.

"True enough. Well, Shelly's certainly going to have a full house now, isn't she?"

"She was actually worried about being lonely this weekend," I said. "That's not about to happen now, is it?"

"Are you kidding?" Grace asked. "The place is going to be so full of white hats and black ones that there won't be much room left over for anyone else."

"That's okay," I said. "That's all that we need. I for one am glad that we've got so many good guys coming with us this weekend to balance out the potential villains."

"Even though it means putting your mother at possible risk?" Jake asked me.

"Between you, her new husband, and the mayor, I think she's probably going to be safe enough."

"What about me?" Grace asked playfully. "Who's going to be looking after me?"

"Any man with the least sense at all will be doing that," he said.

Grace laughed. "Why, Jake, aren't you the charmer."

"Yes, Jake, you really are," I echoed.

He looked distinctly embarrassed by the exchange, so I decided to take it easy on him. After all, he'd gone out on limb agreeing to come with us this weekend, and I didn't want him to regret it. "Okay," I said, "we've got one way to stir up trouble. What else can we come up with?"

"We have a little more time. Why don't we talk about our suspects and go around the car and say why we think each one of them might have done it?" Grace asked.

I thought that was a great idea, and I was about to start when Jake said, "I don't think so."

"Why not?" I asked him.

"You two can talk all you want to, but I can't just share the information that I've gathered in my official capacity with civilians."

"We won't tell anyone you said anything," Grace said encouragingly.

Jake laughed. "Sorry. We can talk about anything else in the world, but I'm not willing to exchange what I've learned so far just yet."

"If you won't talk, then we won't, either," Grace

said, and then she turned to me. "Right, Suzanne?"

"The rain is really starting to pound down," I said as I glanced out the front windshield. It had been coming down the entire trip up the mountain, but it was really picking up steam now.

"Are you just trying to change the subject?" Jake asked me.

"That, too, but it's really pouring up ahead." I peered through the windshield again, and I could see a wave of rain hurtling toward us. My headlights were already on, but I kicked my wiper blades up to their fastest speed and prepared myself for the coming deluge. The Jeep did well in most inclement weather, but I still wanted to be ready for the wall of rain when it hit us.

Thirty seconds later, having a conversation was nearly impossible anyway, as the interior of my car was filled with the sound of rain slamming down on it. I had to focus everything I had to keep us on the road, and thankfully, my passengers didn't even try to engage me in conversation. I was happy that we'd brought my Jeep. I wasn't at all sure that we would have made it in Grace's company car.

The downpour finally eased up a little, and I let out a deep sigh as my grip loosened on the steering wheel. "That was pretty intense."

"We're supposed to get rain all weekend," Jake said.

"How do you know that?"

"I heard it on the news." Jake paused, and then he added, "You know, even if I can't talk about the case, maybe we can brainstorm about some ideas about how we might trap the killer."

"That sounds like fun," Grace said, and she started

throwing out some pretty outlandish ideas.

"Within reason," Jake corrected her with a laugh.

"Oh, I didn't know you were going to limit me. That might take a little more thought."

By the time we got to the lodge, an imposing old log building aptly named Storm Cloud, we had a few other tricks up our sleeves. I wasn't sure if we'd be able to use them all, but it was nice knowing that we were ready to step in and cause a little trouble for our suspects if the need arose.

Chapter 14

"Welcome to Storm Cloud," Shelly said quickly, meeting us as we piled out of the Jeep. In a rush, we started grabbing our overnight bags and running under the cover of the expansive front porch before we got too soaked in the cold rain. Once we were under the safety of the roof, she added, "I'd have had some of my bellboys take those for you, but unfortunately, we're all alone up here."

"Who's going to cook?" Jake asked.

"Oh, I'm quite the little chef, even if I say so myself," she said as she ran a hand through her wet hair. "The pantry's well stocked, so we won't go wanting for food. You might have to pitch in and make a bed or two or even help wash the dishes, though."

"I believe that I can do both of those things with a modicum of skill," he answered.

"Don't worry about it," Shelly said with a hint of a smile. "The dishwasher is automatic, and everybody can make their own beds, as far as I'm concerned. I don't mind pampering my guests, but all four of us know that it's likely that a killer is going to be among us this weekend."

"No one else has beat us here yet, have they?" I asked Shelly as I looked out onto the empty parking lot. There were puddles everywhere, and more were forming by the minute. We were really in the middle of a genuine deluge.

"Not so far. Have you had any late additions to our slate of visitors?"

"Just one," I answered. "Vince Dade decided to

come after all. Is that going to be a problem?"

"No, the room's already set. You know what's so ironic?"

"What's that?" I asked her.

"Chester would have loved this," she said with a sigh.

"I don't understand," Grace said.

"Oh, I don't mean the murder investigation. I'm talking about having so many folks from April Springs coming up here. For some reason, he really loved that town of yours."

"I can testify that there's a lot to be said for the place myself," Jake said softly. I hoped someday that he'd settle there, maybe even sooner rather than later, but it wasn't anything that I would ever ask him about. If he didn't know that he was welcome, in my cottage as well as my town, then I wasn't exactly sure how else I could show it.

"Is that safe?" I asked as I looked at the stream running beside the road. It was clearly beginning to expand its way toward us, and it didn't look as though it would take a lot more precipitation to push it over its banks.

"Don't worry. It's flooded a few times in the past, but we'll have to get a lot more rain for it to do that again."

"That's exactly what we're supposed to be getting," Jake said ominously.

Grace broke in, holding her cell phone in the air and waving it around. "I can't get a signal."

"And you're probably not going to, either," Shelly said. "This place is pretty remote, but don't worry, we have a landline if you need it."

"Does that mean that there's no Internet?" she asked in obvious distress.

"We're a mountain getaway, after all," Shelly said. "It's a place where you're meant to get in touch with yourself, not the rest of the world."

"Okay," she said reluctantly. "If you say so." Grace tucked her phone back into her purse, and I could see that she was having second thoughts about my idea. I wasn't all that dependent on the Internet myself, but even I liked to touch base with the outside world every now and then. Maybe it would give us the opportunity to focus more on our suspects than anything else.

"So, where are we staying?" I asked as we walked into the lobby, a large expanse enclosed by thick honey-stained logs. A massive stone fireplace occupied the center of the room, and the check-in desk was off to one side. A fire was blazing in the hearth, and I could feel some of the heat coming off it. That was how it should be, in my opinion.

"Let me grab you all some keys," Shelly said. As she handed them out, she explained, "Grace, you're in #10." After she handed the key to my best friend, she said, "I put the Hoffs in #1, Kevin Leeds in #2, and I left #3 open for Vince Dade. Then #4 is for Chief Martin and Dot, while #5 is for the mayor. That leaves 6, 7, 8, and 9. Would the two of you be needing one room, or two?"

It was so discreet a way to ask if Jake and I would be sharing a room that it was all I could do not to laugh. Instead of answering her directly, I turned to my boyfriend and looked at him expectantly. He took the hint, and then he answered for himself. "Better give me #6 and put Suzanne in #9."

"Are you trying to shield me from the killer?" I asked Jake, amused that he'd put himself as far away from me as he could with the rooms that Shelly had left. Was he honestly afraid of what my mother might think? I was a grown woman, divorced and living on my own again, but even if none of that were true, there was nothing that said I had to stay in the room that had been assigned to me.

"No, but I'm probably going to be keeping some strange hours while we're here, so it's probably best this way. Is that all right with you?"

"Hey, if she gets lonely, she can always come bunk with me," Grace said with a laugh.

"Be careful. I might just take you up on that," I said.

"My door's always open, especially since my boyfriend is back in April Springs keeping the town safe from armed desperados."

"I don't know about that," Jake said, "but he does have a lot on his plate at the moment, even without the murder investigation. It's not easy overseeing an entire town, something that he's about to find out for himself."

"Are you saying that I'd just be a distraction if I were back there with him?" Grace asked, clearly enjoying baiting my boyfriend a little.

I would have stepped in and stopped it, but Jake was perfectly capable of handling things himself. All I did was step back and enjoy the show. "Grace, you know as well as I do that you can be a distraction wherever you are."

My best friend turned to me and asked with a wink, "Suzanne, is your boyfriend actually flirting with me?"

"Not that I could tell," I said with a smile. "He's just

telling the truth. You do seem to get more than your share of attention."

"Can I help it if I'm interesting?" she asked with a smile.

"Sure, let's call it interesting," I said as I laughed.

Shelly was clearly uncertain about what to make of our playful sparring. "May I show you to your rooms?"

"Don't worry. We can find them ourselves," I said as I grabbed my key. "After all, you've got to get ready for your other guests."

"I've got plenty of time," Shelly said. "After all, they aren't due to arrive for another hour."

That's when we heard a car horn outside in the parking lot.

Evidently someone had decided to get there early.

That meant that the show was about to start.

I just hoped that my plan worked. At its best, we'd catch a murderer, but at its worst, someone who was innocent might die.

The odds weren't bad, but the stakes were high. But in the end, I knew that it was the only game in town, and I honestly believed that we didn't have any other choice.

One way or the other, we were committed now.

Chapter 15

"Do you honestly expect us to carry our own bags?"
Maggie Hoff asked as she burst in through the front
door of the lodge. She was soaked from the brief dash
to cover, and the woman looked perfectly miserable. "I
should have known that this 'free' trip was going to be
worth every penny that it's costing us."

"We're shorthanded, it's true," Shelly said evenly,
"but that doesn't mean that you can't enjoy your stay
with us."

"Enjoyment was never offered to us as part of the
deal," Maggie said as she glanced over at me. "What
on earth is keeping my husband?"

Nathan came in a little less animated than his wife
had been, but that was perfectly understandable, given
the fact that he was weighed down by five pieces of
not-insubstantial luggage. "Where should I put these?"
he asked as he started to set the bags down on the
lobby floor.

"I'll be glad to show you to your room," Shelly said
as she grabbed their key.

Maggie didn't look very pleased about that, and I
had to wonder if she'd been hoping for a room by
herself. We could have easily accommodated her, but
that wouldn't have allowed us to add the extra
pressure of having her in such close proximity to her
husband. That probably wouldn't be that big an issue
for most couples, but we knew that Maggie had been
cheating on Nathan with Chester for quite some time. I
had to wonder if they shared a bedroom at home, but
they weren't going to have any choice here. I knew lots

of married couples that enjoyed their own private spaces when it came to sleep, and I had to wonder how it would impact these two being jammed together in a single room.

As Shelly led them to their accommodations, I asked Jake, "Is the fact that they showed up early going to influence our plans any?"

"Well, I was hoping to get a better idea of the hotel layout before our first suspects arrived, but we'll find a way to deal with it," Jake acknowledged.

Grace chimed in. "There are guest rooms, a dining room, a kitchen, and this lobby. What else do you need to know?"

"You just mentioned the main rooms," Jake said, "but I've seen at least five other doors that I don't know what they're hiding. Let's not forget that a killer is going to be staying here with us this weekend. The more information I have about this place, the better I can prepare myself."

"Don't worry," I said as I patted his arm. "We'll get a tour from Shelly as soon as the Hoffs are in their room. I'm sure that they're going to at least want to change into dry clothes, so that should give us some time to scope out the lay of the land."

"Okay, I can live with that," Jake said as we both spotted Grace waving her cellphone around as though it were a flag in a Fourth of July parade. "Shelly already told you that there was no signal up here."

"She could be wrong, couldn't she?" Grace asked as she continued to search for a signal. "This phone is the latest thing in personal communication devices, and the guy who sold it to me said that I could pick up a tower practically anywhere." After trying in vain for another few seconds, she put it back in her purse and added, "Apparently not here, though."

"It's okay," I said calmly, trying to reassure her. "The world will keep on spinning, even if we're a bit out of touch with it at the moment."

"That remains to be seen," Grace said.

Shelly rejoined us with the hint of a smile on her lips.

"What's so funny?" I asked her.

"Not funny, really, just amusing. Apparently the missus isn't pleased with her accommodations."

"What did she expect?" I asked.

"I'm guessing five-star treatment and a wing to herself at a minimum," Shelly said. "Not to worry. I've dealt with her type before. I can handle her."

"You never finished your tour," Jake reminded her.

"Okay, but we'll have to make it quick. Nathan warned me that the rest of our suspects would probably show up early as well."

"How could he possibly know that?" Grace asked her.

"Evidently the Hoffs saw Vince Dade and Kevin Leeds both filling up at the gas station at the bottom of the hill."

"Were they together?" I asked.

"No, not from the sound of it. Still, we don't have much time. Okay, here goes. That door is a broom closet, and this one leads to the mechanical room," she said as she pointed to the two closest doors to us.

"What about the others?" Jake asked.

"The third room in line is where we keep some of our overflow supplies like toilet paper, tissues, and paper towels, and the next door goes down to the bomb shelter."

"You've actually got a bomb shelter on site here?" I asked her.

"It's really just for storms, but I've called it the bomb shelter forever, so the name kind of stuck."

"Is there any chance that I could look around down there?" Jake asked.

"Not unless you can swim," Shelly said with a bit of a frown. "When we have a heavy rain like today, it starts filling up with overflow water from the stream."

"How can it be called a storm shelter if it does that?" I asked her.

"That's kind of why I call it a bomb shelter. As a storm shelter, it's a real bomb. Get it?"

"Okay, what else have we missed?" Jake asked, ignoring her attempt at humor.

Shelly thought about it a moment, and then she explained, "There's just one more door down here that you haven't seen yet. That's another closet that houses all of our games."

"Do you mean like board games?" I asked her.

"Those are there, but we have some outside sports as well, like badminton, volleyball, just general summer-camp kind of stuff. To be honest with you, it's a huge closet, and I haven't inventoried it forever. It's hard to say what exactly is in there at the moment. The previous owners were pack rats, and cleaning that room out was one job that I just never got around to."

"I'll check it out later," Jake said. "One more thing. I've noticed that you have candles and flashlights stashed all over the place. Do you lose power a lot here?"

Shelly nodded. "More than I'd like. The problem is that our power lines come in through the trees, and sometimes trees are taken down in storms."

"Why don't you have buried cables?" I asked her.

"Too expensive," she explained. "We're running on a razor-thin profit margin here as it is, so we save money every way that we can. I hope this was a good idea inviting everyone up here during a storm," Shelly added, and for the first time since we'd arrived, she looked a little concerned about the situation we'd created.

"Don't worry. I'm sure that it's all going to turn out fine," I said.

"Let's see," Jake said with the hint of a smile. "We've invited a murderer to join us up here, along with three other people we suspect are capable of committing the crime, and more innocent folks are joining us as well. There's a storm raging outside, the basement is filling up with water, not to mention the overflowing stream just outside the front door, and the power is questionable at best. Sure, you're right. What could possibly go wrong?"

"That's what I'm talking about," Grace said with a laugh. "Jake, I didn't know that sarcasm was one of your verbal weapons of choice, but I like it."

He chose to ignore her comment. "Like I said before, we need to be ready for anything."

"Don't worry so much. We're ready," I said, though I was less confident than I might have sounded. I had been concerned about my plan before, but when Jake laid all of the perils out so succinctly, it sounded a bit like sheer lunacy to me now.

Jake was about to respond when the front door opened again, and I watched as Vince Dade struggled to close it when Kevin Leeds swept in behind him.

"Hey, watch it," Kevin said as he entered the lodge.

"Sorry," Vince said, though he didn't sound as though he was sorry at all. "I didn't see you there."

"How bad is it getting out there?" Shelly asked a little anxiously.

"I followed this guy up the road," Kevin said as he pointed to Vince Dade. "If I hadn't been on his bumper the entire time, I don't think I would have made it."

"You could have always turned back," Vince said as he took his hat off and shook it off, water flying everywhere as he did it.

"Are you telling me that you didn't see the road behind us as we drove in?" Kevin asked him incredulously. "You're kidding, right?"

"What about the road?" Shelly asked him, clearly concerned about the situation.

"I got through just before a surge of water took it out. The stream jumped the banks, and everything is flooded behind us. There's no way that anyone without a boat is going to get through that mess now."

I knew what that meant without anyone spelling it out for me.

Grace, Jake, and I were alone with our suspects. While Shelly wasn't at the top of our list, her alibi still hadn't been confirmed, and there was no way that was going to happen now. It would be too easy to assume that she was innocent of Chester's murder, but that wouldn't do any of us any good. I hadn't liked the odds all that much before when we thought we'd have Chief Martin, my mother, and George Morris with us, but suddenly, there were more bad guys than good ones staying at the lodge.

"How long do you think that the road will be

closed?" Jake asked, clearly thinking the same thing that I had.

"If it stopped raining right now, it probably wouldn't be crossable until tomorrow afternoon," Shelly said as the Hoffs decided to join us.

"And if it doesn't stop anytime soon?" I asked her.

"It might take a while longer than that," Shelly acknowledged.

At that moment, there was a tremendous crack of lightning outside, followed almost instantly by the resounding blast of thunder, and every light in the place went out as the rain continued to beat down on the lodge roof, sending a staccato echo of sound through the room that unhappily reminded me of gunfire.

It appeared that we were really in for it now.

Chapter 16

"Everybody needs to calm down," Shelly said as all
of our suspects gathered near the big fireplace in the
lobby. It was generating most of the light we had
available to us now, and all of the warmth. "We're
prepared for just such situations as this here at the
lodge, so there's no need for anyone to panic."

"That's easy for you to say," Nathan Hoff replied.

"Nathan, hush," his wife, Maggie, said, almost
without conscious thought. I had a hunch that
shushing him was as automatic to her as breathing was.

"The first thing we need to do is for everyone to take
a flashlight," Shelly said as she leaned forward and
picked up a large wicker basket full of a variety of
flashlights.

"There's some light coming from the fire," Vince
said. "Why do we need flashlights of our own?"

"Because everywhere else in the lodge is going to be
unlit, so unless you plan on staying right here the entire
time, you're going to need a way to see."

Kevin Leeds took a light, tested it, and then he said,
"Thanks, Shelly."

"You're welcome," she answered. Everyone took a
flashlight, including Jake, Grace, and me. I flicked
mine on once and found a bright, strong beam. Good.
It appeared that at least mine had fresh batteries in it.

"Now, if you'll all have a seat near the fire," Shelly
said, "I'll go over some of the things that you'll need to
know while the power is out."

There was ample seating around the hearth, so we all
took seats, though I noticed that Jake chose a spot in

back where he could watch everyone else without being easily observed himself. I was happy that he was on the case, but I wouldn't have minded all of us having some backup. That was just wishful thinking, though. Nobody was getting through that flood. I had to focus on what we had, and that wasn't entirely inconsequential. While Jake was the only official law enforcement officer present, Grace and I were not entirely without skills of our own.

After everyone was seated, our hostess moved closer to the fire and began to speak. "You should all know that the lodge is prepared for any emergency, not that this qualifies as one. It's mostly just going to be a minor inconvenience."

"When will the power be restored?" Maggie asked.

"Doesn't this dump have a generator?" Vince asked belligerently.

"I don't want to be here anymore," Nathan added.

The statement and questions came close enough together so that Shelly didn't have time to answer one before someone else spoke up. "I'll answer your questions, but then I'd appreciate it if you'd let me finish speaking before you ask any more. Agreed?"

There were a few reluctant nods around the room, and she took the following silence as agreement. "The power, as well as the road, will most likely be restored sometime tomorrow or the next day," Shelly said as she glanced from Maggie Hoff to her husband. "A great deal of that depends on the severity of the storm, and how much longer we're in for it." She then turned to Vince. "We've never seen a reason to have a generator, not that we could have afforded one if we'd wanted it. Besides, sometimes this is a part of the whole experience."

"What are we going to do for food while we're waiting for the flood waters to recede?" Vince asked, ignoring her request to hold all questions until the end.

"There are no worries there. We have propane for our stove, and plenty of hot water, as well."

"But no lights?" Nathan asked timidly.

"Just the flashlights in your hands."

"What about candles?" Maggie asked. "I see them all over the place."

"If you'll look carefully, you'll see that nearly all of them are decorative and have never even been lit."

"Why is that?" Grace asked, clearly curious herself.

Shelly shrugged. "This place is constructed almost entirely of wood. One errant candle could light the entire lodge on fire. If that happened, then we'd be forced out into the elements with no immediate hope of rescue, so I think it's best if we all just stick with flashlights." She smiled a little in the flickering light coming from the fireplace, and I was surprised by just how dark it had gotten so quickly. Though it was late afternoon, we should have still been getting plenty of sunlight, which we probably would have if it hadn't been for the storm clouds that were still pelting us with rain.

"I guess that explains why the place is called Storm Cloud," Kevin said.

"We're in a valley where clouds move in and stay sometimes," Shelly explained. "I've personally always liked the drama of the name."

"Well, it's fitting, I'll give you that," Vince said. He looked around and asked, "Where's your staff, by the way? Shouldn't they be here to take care of us?"

"Unfortunately, my people are taking a much-needed break at the moment," she answered. "We'll each have to pitch in if we're going to get through this with the minimum of unpleasantness."

"I don't know about the rest of you, but I for one am hungry," Kevin Leeds said. "You said the stove was working, but who's going to do the cooking if your staff is gone?"

"I'm going to do it myself," she said. "As a matter of fact, if you'll excuse me, I'll go to the kitchen right now and start working on our next meal."

Jake whispered something to Grace, who nodded and stood up as well. "I'll give you a hand."

"Thank you, but it's really not necessary," Shelly replied.

"Maybe not, but just think about how much fun we can have if we work together."

Shelly shrugged. "Fine, if that's what you want to do. Follow me."

"What are the rest of us supposed to do in the meantime?" Vince asked curtly.

"You could always play a game while we're cooking," Grace said.

"What kind of game did you have in mind?" Nathan asked her.

"I saw Clue earlier," she answered.

No one in the room thought that was very funny, but if it dampened Grace's spirits any, she didn't show it. For my best friend, life was a game to be enjoyed, and sometimes I envied her that attitude.

After Grace and Shelly disappeared into the kitchen, I moved to Jake and asked softly, "Why did you send her after Shelly?"

"No one should be alone right now," he said just as softly.

"That's a good idea," I answered as I moved a little closer to him.

"I'm not playing a stupid child's board game, but that doesn't mean that I want to just sit here and wait for our meal either," Maggie said to no one in particular.

Jake took the opportunity to speak, and when he did, all gazes turned directly to him. "We can go about our business and do the things we need to do despite the lack of electricity."

"Do you honestly want to grill us while the world's coming down around us outside?" Vince asked with a sneer.

"You're being a little overdramatic, but think of it that way if you want to."

"How do *you* think of it?" Maggie asked him.

"I'd like to believe that I'm here to help you eliminate yourselves as murder suspects," he replied. "I don't see why a lack of electricity should stop us from doing that."

"You mean that you're going to try to eliminate all but one of us," Vince replied as he stared hard at my boyfriend.

"That's right. All but one," Jake repeated. "I'm going to be holding the interviews in the dining room, one at a time, so we might as well get started. Now, who wants to go first?"

"If you ask me, this is all utter nonsense, but if we must, we must. There's just one condition," Maggie said. "My husband and I will speak to you together."

"No, you won't," Jake said firmly. There was clearly

no room for disobedience in his voice. For a second I thought Maggie was going to fight him on it, but after a moment's hesitation, she nodded. "Very well. Let's get this nonsense over with. I'll go first." Without waiting for Jake to answer, she stood and walked past him on her way to the dining room, turning her flashlight on as she left the light from the fire.

Before Jake joined her, he told the rest of the group, "I'd appreciate it if none of you wanders off. This shouldn't take long, and I don't want to have to go looking for you. Is that understood?"

The three men remaining clearly didn't like his orders, but they didn't dare cross him either, so they all reluctantly agreed.

I started to follow Jake into the dining room when he stopped and turned to me. In a soft voice, he said, "Suzanne, I'm truly sorry, but I need you to stay here and watch the rest of them for me."

"I can do that," I said, though I had really wanted to be in that room with him. This weekend wasn't about what I wanted, though.

"Thanks," he said with a grateful smile.

Maggie paused at the door, then turned and looked at us with a frown. "Well? Are we doing this, or not?"

"I'm coming," Jake said.

I didn't envy him one little bit. Maggie Hoff could be wholly unpleasant when she wanted to be, and I had a hunch that she wasn't going to take it easy on Jake during their interview.

Perhaps I was in the right room after all.

Three minutes after Maggie and Jake closed the door, Vince Dade stood up from his seat.

"Where are you going?" I asked him.

"I need to find a bathroom," he said.

"Jake asked you to stay here."

"I heard him," Vince said as he shook his head and started to walk away.

I wasn't about to let that happen, so I stood up and followed him. I caught up with Vince out of earshot of everyone else. "Hang on a second."

He clearly didn't like the fact that I was following him. "What do you want, Suzanne?"

"Aren't you afraid of looking guilty, running away like this?"

"I didn't do it, so that's not an issue," Vince said.

"Why should anyone believe you?"

Vince looked around, and then, his voice a near whisper, he said, "If you tell anyone this I'll call you a bald-faced liar, but Chester didn't hurt me one bit by pulling out of that deal, and neither did your mother or the police chief."

"I find that hard to swallow," I said. "You were angry, and everybody in town knew it."

"That's because that's what they were supposed to think, you idiot," he snarled. "That deal was meant to fail from the outset. I had way too many investors to ever pay off if it succeeded. All Chester did was give me a public way of wailing about how much I'd lost." The man's wicked grin wasn't lost on me. "I might have lost a little capital when the three of them pulled out of the deal, but I gained a world of credibility from it, and I milked it for every ounce I could squeeze out of it. Now leave me alone."

Vince stormed away, and I was too dumbstruck to even protest. Could it possibly be true? If it were, it would explain a lot.

When I got back to the lounge area, I took my seat again.

"Well, that went well, didn't it?" Kevin said with the hint of a smile. "Don't worry about Vince. He's been in a bad mood since the day he was born."

"Have you known him that long?" I asked the bank clerk.

"Sometimes it feels as though I have," he said.

Even though Jake was interrogating suspects in the other room, there was no reason that I couldn't ask a question or two of my own. "How long did you know Chester?"

"Almost as long as I've known Vince," he replied. "That's why I'm so happy that we finally patched things up between us. It took until the day he died, but he made things right with me."

"Did he really pay off that ten dollars?"

"As a matter of fact, he did," Kevin answered with a smile as he dug out his wallet. He selected a bill and handed it to me. In the flickering light from the fire, I read where someone had written, *"This is my acknowledgment that all debts I have ever owed to Kevin Leeds have now been paid in full."*

It was signed Chester A. Martin.

As Kevin took it back, he said, "Chester told me the day he died that he was going to start fresh, and getting rid of his debt to me was just one of the things he was going to do before he started his new life."

"What else was he planning on doing?" I asked.

"I have no idea. I'm just glad I got this," Kevin said as he tucked the bill back into his wallet. It might just

be the only ten-dollar bill he'd ever held in his hands
that would never get spent.

"How about you, Nathan?" I asked the remaining
suspect there. "How long did you know Chester?"

"As a matter of fact, I didn't know the man at all."

His answer surprised me. "Really? April Springs is
a pretty small place. How could your paths not have
crossed in all of the years that you've lived here?"

Nathan hastily explained, "I don't mean that I didn't
know who he was, I was just saying that we never had
a personal relationship other than nodding to each
other on the street. Suzanne, there are a great many
folks in town that I don't interact with on a daily basis."

"Didn't you ever go to the library?" Kevin asked
him.

"I've never been much for reading," Nathan said.
"Sports are my things." It figured. He was a washed-
up football player, so I didn't have any problem
believing that was what he was interested in.

"You know, there are a great many excellent books
written about sports," Kevin said.

"I like to watch them on television, not read about
them," Nathan replied. Evidently he was a man of
limited attention span. That wasn't a requirement to
watch sports, though. Jake loved to read, but he also
enjoyed watching football, so I knew that the two
weren't mutually exclusive, but evidently they were in
Nathan Hoff's mind. I watched the men as they spoke.
Kevin had a small silver rectangle in his hands, and he
was flipping it back and forth as he talked. It slipped
for a moment and tumbled out of his hands, and before
he could scoop it up again, I realized that it was a
cigarette lighter, something I hadn't seen in a while. I

was about to look away when I noticed what was engraved on the side of it. BURN BABY BURN was etched there, along with a silhouette of flames. He grabbed it up and shoved it into his pockets, but I wasn't going to let it go at that.

"That's an unusual object you've got there," I said to him.

"What's that?"

"Your lighter."

He shrugged. "It was a gift. I don't even smoke anymore, but I still like to carry it around with me."

"May I ask where you got it?"

Instead of answering me, he stood and started to pace. "How long is this going to take, anyway?"

"Why, do you have something better to do?" Nathan asked him wryly. "Is there a book you're just dying to read?"

"Nathan, I don't know why you're not more worried than you appear to be," Kevin replied.

"Why should I be concerned about anything?"

"Oh, I don't know, maybe because your wife is in there talking to a cop about the possibility that she's a murderer?" Kevin asked.

"Believe me when I tell you that my wife is more than capable of taking care of herself," Nathan said.

"Whatever," Kevin replied.

I was about to say something when the dining room door opened and Maggie came storming out. She was tucking something back into her purse as she raced out. What was it, a parking ticket or something? I wanted to ask her about it, but this wasn't the time or the place.

"We're not finished, Maggie," Jake said as he followed her out of the dining room.

"You may not be, but I am," she said. "Nathan, we're going to our room."

To my surprise, her husband didn't budge. "Sorry, but I can't do that. The inspector hasn't spoken with me yet."

"Actually, right now it's Chief," Jake said. "Come on in, Nathan. You're next."

When the man stood, it was clear that he wasn't even torn about the decision. I watched Maggie closely as her husband left the room. She was clearly unhappy about the situation, but there wasn't much that she could do about it. Maggie stood there a moment longer, and then she hurried down the hallway toward the room she was sharing with her husband.

Kevin watched her go, and I heard him mumble something under his breath.

"Sorry, I didn't quite catch that," I said.

He looked surprised when he realized that I'd been listening. "It was nothing."

"Really? Because it sure didn't sound like nothing from where I was sitting."

Kevin shrugged, and then he explained, "I just said that I was glad that she wasn't my wife. She might be a pretty woman, but I'm willing to bet that she's an absolute pain to live with."

"I'm sure that we all have our moments," I said.

"Maybe, but that's baggage that I wouldn't be willing to carry, no matter how pretty the suitcase was."

Shelly and Grace came out of the kitchen. As the lodge owner looked around the room, she asked, "Where did everybody go?"

"Jake is in the dining room talking to Nathan,

Maggie's in their room, Vince left half an hour ago to find a restroom, and Kevin and I are just sitting here, waiting for Jake. How's it coming in the kitchen?"

"We're still getting things ready," Grace said. "I told Shelly that I wanted to pop in here, and she decided to join me." My friend didn't look all that pleased by the idea, but clearly she hadn't had any say in the matter.

"There will be time to finish prepping the meal later," Shelly said as she took a seat. "Besides, I just wanted to enjoy the fire a little."

I glanced at the fireplace as she added another log to it. "It's quite lovely, isn't it?"

Shelly nodded. "The man who laid it is in his eighties, and he's still working on fireplaces to this day. I met him once in town, and let me tell you, he's quite the character."

Nathan walked out just then, and I realized that his interview had been shorter than the one his wife had gone through. Why was the man's wallet in his hand? What had Jake asked for, his identification, or had Nathan just volunteered something that I'd missed? I couldn't wait to find out what Jake had learned in his interview sessions.

"Finished so soon?" I asked.

"Not exactly. It's more likely just to be continued," Jake said.

Nathan ignored us all. His face was ashen, and his lips were two thin lines. I wasn't sure what Jake had said to him, but it had obviously upset him.

"Let's go, Kevin. Come on in," Jake said, and then he looked around the room. "Where did Vince wander off to?"

"He said that he was going off in search of a

restroom," I said.

"Find him for me, would you? He's next."

"Will do," I said as Kevin walked past Jake into the dining room.

"Would you like some company?" Grace asked me as I headed for the guest rooms.

"Always," I said.

The second we were out of earshot of the others, Grace whispered, "That was weird."

"What part of it? If you ask me, everything that's been happening has been odd."

"I'm talking about my time in the kitchen with Shelly."

"What happened?" I asked.

"Well, first off, she wanted to know everything we'd found out about Chester's murder so far," Grace said.

"That's only natural, isn't it? After all, they were very close."

"That's the thing," Grace explained. "She didn't seem to give a hoot about the other suspects. All she wanted to know was what clues we'd uncovered so far, and what they meant."

"I suppose that makes sense," I said a little uncertainly. "What made it so odd?"

"It was almost as though she expected us to know something that we didn't. I don't know. It felt as though she was trying to hide something from us."

"She wouldn't be the first suspect who did it, and that doesn't even include the killers we've tracked in the past. Sometimes it feels as though everyone we talk to is ashamed of something. It makes it hard to tell the good guys from the bad guys."

"I have a feeling that we're all a little bit of each

one," Grace said.

"Me, too," I agreed.

"Anyway, after that, she disappeared for at least ten minutes looking for some utensil or something in the other room."

"You were supposed to stay together," I reminded her.

"I know that, but I couldn't exactly drop what I was doing and follow her around." Another bolt of lightning hit outside, followed quickly by the roar of thunder. That had been too close for comfort.

"It's not letting up, is it?" she asked me.

"Well, at least it's not snow," I said.

"I'd take that over this," Grace said with a tremor in her voice. "Cold and rain don't mix well in my book. I'd rather be somewhere warm and tropical."

"After this is all over, maybe I'll join you," I said with a smile.

We were at Vince's room now. The door was closed, and I started to knock when Grace reached over and tried the doorknob.

"What are you doing?" I asked her in a soft hiss.

"I just wanted to see if he'd locked it," she said. "He did."

I finished the motion of my knock, but there was no answer from inside.

I repeated it, this time louder and more insistent, but there was still no response.

Was Vince ignoring us, gone, or had something bad happened to him?

No matter what the reason it might be, Grace and I needed to find out which one applied to this situation.

Chapter 17

"What should we do?" Grace asked me. "Should we break the door down?"

"No, we don't need to do anything that drastic just yet. Shelly's bound to have a master key that fits every room in the lodge."

"Good thinking," Grace replied as she started back to the main room.

Shelly was stoking the fire when we walked in. "Do you happen to have a master key to the lodge?" I asked her.

"Of course I do. Why, what's going on?"

"Vince Dade won't answer our knocks," I said.

Shelly frowned for a moment. "Perhaps he's just taking a nap."

"Or maybe it's something more dire than that," Grace suggested. "That's what we're trying to find out."

"Either way, he's not answering our knocks. Could you grab the key and come with us?"

Shelly still wasn't happy about the situation. "Shouldn't we get Jake first and ask him what we should do?"

"Not until we find out what's going on for ourselves," I said firmly. Part of it was that I didn't want to disturb Jake while he was interviewing a suspect, but another part of me realized that it was because Grace and I had started this search together, and we wanted to see it through, no matter what.

"Fine. Let me get my key," she said as she headed off for the kitchen.

"Do you really keep it in there?" I asked her.

"Not in the kitchen itself, but I have a little office off the pantry I like to use sometimes."

"What about the one in the lobby?" I asked her. I'd seen it coming in, a small cubicle-sized room just off the registration area.

"I use that sometimes as well, but most of the real work gets done back here." Shelly made her way through the kitchen, but before she opened the small door near the pantry, she paused, and I saw that it was already partially opened. "That's odd."

"What is?" I asked her.

"This door always stays closed, and I mean always," she said. Shelly seemed almost frightened to open it, so I stepped up and pushed the door all the way open. I was half expecting to see Vince Dade's lifeless body lying on the floor, but there was no sign of a corpse anywhere and no room in the small space to hide one, for that matter.

Shelly stared at an empty nail. "Now I'm really worried." She pointed to the nail as she added, "That's where I keep the master key, and it's gone. Whoever has it can go anywhere they want to in the lodge. No door in the entire place is truly locked now."

Chapter 18

"This is not good," Grace said worriedly.

"You can say that again," I replied, and then I turned back to the lodge owner. "Shelly, are sure that it was there earlier?"

"I never keep it on me," Shelly said. "As a matter of fact, I can't remember the last time I had to use the master key, but I know that it was there this morning, because I saw it hanging from its nail where it always is. What are we going to do now?"

"I think it's time to get Jake," I said.

"Are you sure?" Grace asked me. Clearly she wanted to continue our investigation a little further without my boyfriend, but I knew when it was time to call in reinforcements.

"I'm positive," I said. "Let's go get him."

The three of us walked out of the kitchen and through the main space together, and I knocked firmly on the dining room door.

Jake opened it a minute later, clearly unhappy about me interrupting him. "What is it, Suzanne? Can't it wait?"

"Sorry, but this is important. Vince Dade isn't answering our knocks."

He frowned a little. "Is that all? Maybe he's taking a nap."

"Not after the way we were just knocking," Grace added. "That's not all, though."

"What else happened?" Jake asked.

"The master key is gone," Shelly said. "Someone

must have stolen it in the past couple of hours."

That got Jake's attention. "Are you sure that you didn't just misplace it?"

"I'm positive. I saw it right where it belonged earlier today, and now it's gone."

Jake nodded. "Okay. Don't worry. I'm sure that it will turn up." He turned back to Kevin. "We'll finish this later."

"Fine by me," he said. "If you need me, I'll be in my room, with the door locked." Almost as an afterthought, he added, "Not that it's probably going to do me much good."

We all followed him into the hallway, and Jake knocked on Vince's door himself. After there was no answer, he jiggled the door handle, but it was still locked.

"We already tried that," Grace said.

"And it didn't hurt anything to try it again," Jake said as he turned to Shelly. "Is there any other way into that room without breaking the door down?"

"Not that I know of," she said. "Go on; do what you have to. I can always replace the lock if I have to. Vince might be in trouble in there, and that's all that matters."

"Okay. Everybody stand over there."

Jake braced himself against the wall opposite the door, but instead of using his shoulder as I'd expected, he kicked it solidly right where the latch mechanism met the door.

It opened with a jolt as the door swung open violently on its hinges, and we all looked inside to see what was really going on in Vince Dade's room.

"No one's here," Jake said after he looked carefully around the room and the accompanying bathroom.

"Where could he be, then?" I asked. "It's still storming outside, so I doubt that he just decided to go out for a walk."

"I don't know what to tell you," Jake said as he checked the door that he'd just kicked in. "Sorry about that."

Shelly shrugged. "I've got a man who can fix it. Right now I'm more worried about my guest."

"Where should we look?" I asked her.

"The place isn't all that big," Shelly said. "Let me grab the rest of the room keys. I'd like to search the empty rooms we haven't used, too."

"You do that, and we'll check around ourselves," Grace said.

Jake nodded. "Good enough. I'm going to grab my jacket and head outside."

I could hear the rain pounding down from where I stood. "Are you honestly going out in that?"

"I don't have much choice, Suzanne. If he's not in here, then he's got to be somewhere outside."

"Then I'm going with you," I said firmly.

Jake shook his head, though I could see him trying to hide the hint of a smile. "Thanks, but there's no sense in both of us getting soaked to the bone. Besides, you and Grace need to stay together."

"If I'm watching her back, who's going to be watching yours?" I asked.

"I don't mind being alone, Jake. Suzanne should go with you," Grace answered.

There was a firmer edge to his voice when he spoke again. "As much as I appreciate the concern for my well-being you both are showing, this isn't open for debate."

I knew better than to go against his wishes on this. "Let me at least grab your jacket for you."

"I have boots," Shelly volunteered. "Surely there's a pair that will fit you. They're by the back door. As a matter of fact, that might be a good place to start looking."

Jake didn't need her to fill in the blanks for him. "You're thinking that a pair might already missing."

"It's worth a look," Shelly said, and all four of us hurried to the back door, our flashlights bobbing in an odd pattern.

It surprised me that the other guests hadn't come out when they'd heard Vince's door being broken down. Maybe Nathan and Maggie were too involved in their own drama to pay us any attention, or maybe they just didn't care. It was easy enough to believe that they each had a motive for killing Chester. Infidelity was about as personal an affront as possible in most folks' minds. As for Kevin, who knew what was going on in that man's head? I mean, seriously, who holds a grudge so long over a measly ten bucks, principle or not? He was a bit of a wild card in my mind, and predicting what might or might not drive him to commit murder was beyond me. At least Vince Dade had a solid motive for killing Chester Martin if he'd been lying to me earlier about welcoming a scapegoat for his land-fraud scheme. The entire town believed that he'd been burned, both financially and emotionally, and he might have been out for revenge, no matter how long ago the offense had occurred. But that didn't explain where he was right now, and with this many suspects nearby, I hated the thought of one of them being out of our sight for any appreciable time at all.

"I can't say for sure, but it seems that a pair of men's boots might be missing," Shelly said as she studied the pile of boots jammed into a closet by the back door.

"Can't you say for sure by looking?" Jake asked.

Shelly looked a little embarrassed to admit, "Over the course of a season, you'd be amazed by how many people walk off with our things. On any given day, it's tough to keep an inventory of everything we have on hand with my small staff. We had a guest one year who stole light bulbs, and not just from the room, either. It took me two hours to find all of the empty sockets in the place."

"Then I need to go out and have a look around for myself," Jake said.

I'd stopped long enough to grab Jake's jacket from his room. "Here, take it. You're going to need this."

"And a hat might be in order, too," Shelly said as she grabbed one from a peg on the closet door. "That might help keep you a little dry."

Jake put on his jacket, and after a moment's hesitation, he reluctantly took the hat as well. "If I'm not back in thirty minutes, lock the doors and wait for reinforcements. Somebody's bound to come along sooner or later."

"No," I said. "Sorry, but that's not going to happen."

Jake was displeased with me; it was clear in the way he looked at me, but I wasn't about to back down. "Suzanne, don't forget. I'm the one who is in charge of this investigation."

"I'm not denying it, but if you're one minute late, I'm going to come looking for you, orders or not."

Before Jake could comment, Grace said, "And I'll be right behind her. Honestly, you can't make demands on us if you're not here to enforce them," she said with a grin.

It was touch and go for a few seconds, but Jake finally shrugged. "Then I'll be sure to come back in plenty of time."

"We'll be waiting for you," I said as I kissed him good-bye. It was brief but effective.

"See you soon," he said as he started to open the door.

"One way or another, you can count on it," I answered.

We all watched him fade away into the downpour, his flashlight beam quickly being swallowed up by the gloomy day. The late afternoon was darker than it should have been even with the storm.

Shelly must have been thinking the same thing. "We're perched between two mountains, so our sunlight doesn't last a long time on a good day, and what's going on out there is far from that. I need to grab those keys and check the other rooms. Are you two coming with me?"

When I didn't answer, Grace said, "Suzanne, we're going to drive ourselves crazy if just we stand here by the door waiting for him. That half an hour is going to seem like three days."

"There's only twenty-eight minutes left," I said as I checked my watch.

"Still."

"You're right," I replied. "Let's get busy."

After checking all of the empty guest rooms, we did a thorough search of the rest of the lodge, including the door that led to the storm shelter.

Shelly opened it and played the beam of her flashlight down the stairs, and Grace and I looked down as well.

"Something's wrong, isn't it?" Grace asked.

It was quite an understatement. I could see water already touching the bottom step, seeping in from the outside at an alarming rate. "Has it ever been that high before?" I asked Shelly.

She looked a little pale from the sight of it. "Not since I've owned the place. There's a lot of water down there."

"It won't come up this high," I said, though I wasn't sure of that fact at all.

"I thought if I'd ignore it, it would be fine. Basically I haven't had the money to seal the shelter off, so I've just been hoping that it wouldn't ever come to this. What an idiot I was."

"I'm sure that you did what you could with what you had," I said, trying to be reassuring, but the rising water level worried me, too. What would happen if the rain continued at the pace it was falling now? Would we all be driven out by the rising floodwaters? And what about the stream outside? I was certain that it posed a risk to us as well.

It was a delayed risk, though. We had even more pressing issues now.

Where was Vince, and more importantly, what was keeping Jake? I glanced at my watch for the five thousandth time since he'd left, and I saw that he had only three minutes left before I was going after him.

That depended on if I was going to wait that long for him. I suddenly couldn't stand the thought of Jake being out there somewhere, hurt and helpless, unable to come back. If I gave him the full amount of time that I'd promised to earlier, it might already be too late by the time I got to him. I decided that this time, it would be better to ask for forgiveness than permission.

"I'm grabbing my coat and I'm heading outside," I said.

"But you promised Jake you would wait thirty minutes," Shelly said as she glanced at her watch.

"I'll apologize when I find him," I replied.

"Wait for me, then," Grace said. "I'm going, too."

"You two don't mind if I stay here, do you?" Shelly asked as Grace and I prepared ourselves to go outside.

"This is where you need to be. Somebody has to hold down the fort," I said.

I found a pair of nondescript olive boots that didn't fall off my feet, and Grace grabbed a pair of black boots dappled with daisies. Leave it to her to be stylish even when we were on what I hoped was not a rescue mission.

We never made it outside, though.

Just as we were about to leave, the outside door swung open, and I held my breath, waiting to see who was about to step through.

Chapter 19

"Jake, are you okay?" I asked with relief as I reached for the towel Shelly was holding. "Get out of those wet things."

"I'm fine," he said as he took off his jacket and boots. The hat was missing. "A breeze kicked up and blew that thing right off my head. I'll be glad to replace it once this is all over."

"Don't worry about it, Jake, a guest left it three seasons ago. What's it like out there?"

"It's pretty brutal," he admitted. "It's as bad as we thought. The road's completely gone."

"Do you mean that it's under water?" Grace asked.

"No, I mean that it's gone. The stream took it completely out." He turned to Shelly. "It's not going to be easy to fix it, from the look of it. I've got a hunch that your season is over."

Shelly slumped down a little. "Then so is the lodge."

"Come on. You can always start from scratch next season," I said encouragingly.

"Not without the paying guests I'll have to turn away the rest of this one. I was on the edge of bankruptcy before the storm hit. This storm just drove the last nail in my coffin." She looked around at the old place. "You know what? The bank is welcome to it. I've struggled to make it work for years, but most folks just don't seem to care about the isolation we offer anymore. My sister has been after me to retire to the Outer Banks and come live with her, and I think I'm going to take her up on it when we get out of here."

"Maybe you should sleep on it," I said. "I know that

things look bleak right now, but in the morning light, there might be a way out for you."

"Suzanne, it's okay, really. In a way, it's kind of a relief."

I decided to keep my mouth shut. After all, I knew better than anyone what a thin profit margin most small businesses worked with. If I lost a month's worth of sales, I'd have to shutter Donut Hearts myself.

"That begs one question, though, doesn't it?" Grace asked. "Where's Vince Dade?"

"Well, he didn't walk out of here," Jake said. "I know that for a fact. From the look of it, that road's been gone a while. I suspect it washed out just after he and Kevin made it across."

"So that means that he's somewhere inside the lodge," Shelly said. "I honestly don't know where he might be hiding, though."

"Who says that he's hiding?" Jake asked as he toweled off his hair. "We need to round everybody up and inspect their rooms whether they like it or not."

"What do you expect to find?" Shelly asked, clearly concerned with whatever Jake's answer might be.

"I try not to expect anything," he said. "I deal with facts, not guesses and suppositions. Come on, let's go."

"You three go on. I think I'll hang back and get started on dinner," Shelly said.

I didn't expect Jake to offer any resistance to the idea, but yet again, he surprised me. "If you don't mind, I'd rather you come with us, at least for now."

Shelly looked surprised by his suggestion. "I can assure you that I'm perfectly safe in my own kitchen, Jake."

"You're probably right, but what is it going to hurt

to indulge me?"

She shrugged. "Fine. I suppose that it can wait."

Jake smiled. "Then let's go. Until you hear from me, no one should leave the group."

"Do you think that we're all really in danger?" Shelly asked.

"We'd be fools not to entertain the possibility," Grace replied, and then she looked at me. "What? It's true, isn't it?"

"I never denied it," I said.

"Good," she replied.

"Ladies, if we're finished here, let's get started on the rest of our search," Jake said.

"We're right behind you," I said as Jake headed for Nathan and Maggie Hoff's room first.

I wondered what we might find there, given the way the couple had been interacting since they'd arrived. A murder/suicide wasn't out of the question in my mind, a dark thought indeed.

At least we didn't have to break their door down.

"What can we do for you?" Nathan asked as he opened the door partway.

"Is your wife here with you?" Jake asked him.

"Of course she is. Where else would she be?" A frown crossed his lips. "Why do you ask?"

"We need everyone in the main area by the fireplace right now," Jake ordered.

"Who is it?" we heard Maggie call out from inside the room. "What do they want?" As she got closer to the door, she added, "What is this, a lynch mob?"

"Nobody's going to lynch anyone. We're here for your safety," Jake said.

"Why should I believe you?"

I could see my boyfriend tense a little at her jibe. Like most people, he wasn't all that keen on having his orders challenged. I decided to step in before things escalated. "Maggie, the road is gone, and it's hard to say when we'll ever get out of here. We're trying to figure things out."

"Are you telling me that we're trapped?" Her voice was shrill, and Jake glanced back at me. I was expecting some sort of reprimand, but instead, he just smiled.

"I wouldn't put it quite that way," Jake told her.

"How else could you possibly see this situation?" she asked him.

Jake replied, "I'm sure that it's only temporary, but for the time being, we're all sticking together."

"Where are Vince and Kevin, then?" Nathan asked Jake as he looked at us all milling about in the hallway.

"That's what we're trying to figure out," Grace said. "This is Kevin's door, right?" she asked.

"It is," Shelly replied.

Before Jake could say anything, she knocked loudly on it.

Kevin opened the door after a full minute, and from his disheveled appearance, if I had to guess, I'd say that he'd been napping when Grace had knocked. "What's going on?"

"There's a meeting in the lobby by the big fireplace," she said. "Come on."

"Not interested," he said as he tried to close the door.

Jake reached out from beyond Kevin's line of sight and grabbed the door before it could close. "That wasn't a request."

Kevin looked as though he wanted to protest further, but something about Jake's tone of voice must have told him that would be fruitless. "Fine. Give me a second."

"Take all the time you need," Jake said. "We'll wait."

Kevin shrugged, and as he tried to close his door, Jake kept his grip on it firmly. "Do whatever you need to, but this stays open."

"I have to take a leak, okay?" Kevin asked, letting some of his irritation slip through.

"I don't care what you do, but this door isn't closing," Jake said.

"Oh, forget it," Kevin said angrily. "I'll do it later."

Jake just shrugged, clearly not caring one way or the other.

"That just leaves our original missing guest," Shelly said. "And honestly, I can't imagine where Vince might be."

"Are you telling us that he still hasn't shown up?" Maggie asked.

"Do you see him anywhere?" Kevin asked, openly sassing her. Was that a smile that crossed Nathan's lips for a moment? I doubted that he'd ever had the guts to respond to his wife that way, but it appeared that he enjoyed it when someone else did.

"He's probably out there somewhere," Maggie said as she waved a hand toward a window. I glanced out and saw that the rain was still pounding down, and I wondered what the water level in the storm shelter was doing. In a way, I was almost afraid to think about it.

"He's not, though," Jake said.

"How can you possibly know that, Inspector?" Maggie demanded to know.

"It's Chief," Jake said, "and I know because we're on our own little island now with the way the stream has cut us off. It didn't take that long to check; trust me."

"Then logic demands that he's in here somewhere," Kevin said.

"I'm not disagreeing with you," Jake said, "but where?" He turned to Shelly and asked, "Are you absolutely certain that you've checked every place in the lodge where someone might be hiding?"

"I assure you, we've searched it all." Almost as an afterthought, she added, "Everywhere but my bedroom, of course, and I can assure you that he's not in there."

"Let's go look anyway," Jake said. "Where exactly is it?"

"I was teasing," Shelly said. "Surely you don't think that Vince is holed up in my room."

"Well, he has to be somewhere. Just indulge me, okay?"

"Are we all going?" Grace asked.

"Why not?" I replied. "The more the merrier."

There were a few grumbles, but everyone knew that arguing with Jake was going to be pointless, so we all followed Shelly as she led the way through the kitchen and around the far hallway to a small set of stairs. I'd missed them completely before. Once we were all upstairs, I saw that a small door had been tucked into one eave.

Shelly unlocked her door and swung it open. "See? There's no one here."

She was about to close it again when I thought I saw

something — or someone — move on the floor.

Chapter 20

"Hang on," I said as I hurried past Shelly to verify what I thought I'd just seen.

Lying on the floor beside the bed and away from the line of sight through the doorway, I found Vince Dade.

He was tied up, there was duct tape across his mouth, and he appeared to be as mad as a wet cat, but at least he was still alive.

Chapter 21

"I'm not going to lie to you. This is going to sting a little," Jake said as he reached down and ripped the duct tape off Vince's mouth in one swift motion.

"Oww!" Vince shouted. The ropes holding him were fairly loose, and it appeared that he'd nearly worked his way free by the time we'd found him. I finished untying them for him, and his first action was to rub his mouth carefully. "I'm going to kill whoever did this to me."

"Does that mean that you didn't see who tied you up?" I asked. If Jake minded me butting in, he didn't say anything. Clearly he was just as curious about the answer to my question himself.

"I didn't see a thing. Whoever did it hit me from behind," Vince said with disgust as he felt the back of his head and tried to stand. He didn't make it all the way, and ended up sitting down hard on Shelly's bed.

Jake tenderly probed the spot himself, and Vince winced a little as he did. "Hey, take it easy."

"Sorry," Jake said, but there was no sincerity in the apology. "What were you doing up here in the first place? Nobody attacked you and then dragged you up the stairs, I'm pretty sure of that."

Vince looked a little guilty as he finally managed to stand up and explained, "I thought Shelly might have a two-way radio or something up here. I wanted out of here, and I didn't know what else to do."

"You could have just asked me instead of breaking into my room," Shelly said with a frown.

"He didn't have to break in," I said, and then I stared

hard at the man. "Come on. Hand it over, Vince."

"I don't know what you're talking about," he said glumly.

"The master key," I insisted as I held out my hand.

"Fine. You can have it, for all of the good that it did me," he said, but as he reached into his pocket, he suddenly frowned. "You're kidding me."

"You don't have it?" Jake asked.

"Oh, I admit that I had it at one time, but whoever clobbered me must have taken it when I was out cold."

"This is not good," Grace said softly. Her words had more impact than if she'd shouted them, but it wasn't anything that the rest of us weren't feeling as well.

"What are we supposed to do now?" Maggie asked gently. There was softness, a real sense of vulnerability in her voice that I hadn't heard before. The woman was clearly frightened, and why wouldn't she be? We were stranded out in the wilderness with a killer, and there looked to be little hope that we'd manage to get away before something else very bad happened to at least one of us.

"We need to reconvene downstairs," Jake said. "There's not enough room in here for all of us. Can you make it on your own, Vince, or do you need some help?"

"I'll manage," he growled out, so we all headed downstairs. As Vince started to move, though, he headed straight for Kevin Leeds before he could get away. "You did this to me, didn't you?" Vince asked fiercely as he punched the man's chest with a meaty index finger.

"I didn't do a thing to you," Kevin protested. "Have you lost your mind?"

"Then it must have been you!" Vince said as he spun and grabbed Nathan's shirt front instead.

"I don't know what you're talking about," Nathan said as he tried to free himself from Vince's grip.

"Get your hands off my husband this instant," Maggie ordered.

"Why, are you the one who clobbered me? It could have been a woman, and it wouldn't surprise me one little bit if it was you," Vince snapped at her.

"Enough!" Jake ordered, and then he got really close to Vince before he spoke again. "If you don't get yourself under control, I'm going to tie you up myself and gag you with more than duct tape. Is that clear?"

Vince bristled a little at the threat, but then he relaxed a touch. "Fine. I'm okay."

"I mean it, Vince," Jake said strongly.

"Let's just all go downstairs," Vince suggested. It was clear that he was still angry, but it was just as obvious that he thought he'd have better luck confronting members of our group later. I really couldn't blame him. If someone had conked me on the head, tied me up, and taped my mouth shut, I'd be pretty upset about it, too.

Downstairs, we all found spots near the fireplace just as Jake had suggested.

It was growing late in the day now, and full darkness was nearly upon us. The flickering light from the fireplace cast ghostly shadows across the room. In a different set of circumstances, it might have been delightful, but there was an ominous feeling to the moment that carried a sense of foreboding, and there was nothing more that I wished for than being far, far away from this lodge prison.

"I'm hungry," Nathan said after a few moments. "Is anyone else hungry?"

"This is no time to think about food," Maggie scolded her husband.

"I've been wanting to eat for what feels like hours," Kevin Leeds replied.

Maggie shook her head in disgust as she looked at Kevin, but he just smiled in response.

"Why don't I go ahead and fix us something tasty that's quicker than what I had in mind before?" Shelly asked as she stood. "We can eat in an hour."

"If you go, then we all go," Jake said. "No one's leaving my sight."

"What if we have to go to the can?" Kevin asked. "Are you coming then, too?"

"What's wrong, do you have a shy bladder?" Vince asked him, clearly taunting the man a little.

"No, but that doesn't mean that I like an audience, either," Kevin said, and then he turned to Jake. "So, what about it?"

"The men will go together, and the women will do the same thing," he said.

"Well, I'm going right now," Kevin said as he stood.

"Ladies, should we go as well?" Grace asked.

"Why not?" I asked. "Let's reconvene in the kitchen, okay? We all need to eat something, and the sooner the better."

"See you there in a few minutes," Jake said to me, and then we split off into two groups.

Fifteen minutes later, we were all gathered in the kitchen. Camp lights illuminated the working surfaces, but there was darkness everywhere else, and to my surprise, I found myself missing the light from the fireplace in the other room.

"This is going to be challenging," Shelly said as she surveyed her workspace.

"We don't have to have anything elaborate. Do you have the makings for sandwiches?" Jake asked her. "I'm talking cold cuts, peanut butter, and bread. That's all we need."

"Certainly, but I can do much better than that, given a little time," Shelly said.

"Do I have to remind you that we aren't at summer camp or off on some kind of corporate retreat? Anybody who doesn't want a sandwich can just go without eating," Jake said curtly.

"Fine. I have bottles of water and soda as well. You're right. That's probably best. Let me at least set up a buffet line."

I could see that Jake was about to protest, but apparently this wasn't a battle worth fighting. "Okay, but make it quick, okay?" I noticed that he was trying to watch everyone in the place at the same time, an impossible task in the broad light of day, let alone this shadow-filled room. I tried to help, but I could barely keep my focus on one person before another one moved.

After Shelly was satisfied with her offerings, including three types of bread, every condiment known to man, a nice spread of chips and vegetables, and a deli platter full of cold cuts and cheeses, we were ready to eat.

I noticed that there were nice plates at the head of the line, and I commented about them to her.

"Just because we're eating picnic food doesn't mean we have to use paper plates," she said. "Don't you approve?"

"On the contrary, I think it's a nice touch."

I hung back with Jake, and we watched as each guest went through the line. When it was just Jake, Grace, Shelly, and me, I whispered, "Did you find anything out in your interviews?"

"We'll talk about it later," he said. "Would you mind making me a sandwich when you make yours so I can go keep an eye on them? You know what I like."

"I'd better by now," I said with a smile. "Go on."

"Thanks," Jake said, and then he took the time to give me a quick peck on the lips before he rejoined the others.

After he was gone, Shelly said, "He really loves you, doesn't he?"

"Believe me, the feeling is mutual," I said as I started building our sandwiches.

"So why doesn't he propose already?" Shelly asked.

Grace nearly dropped her plate when Shelly said that. She looked at me with a straight face as she asked, "That's a good question, Suzanne. Why hasn't your long-term boyfriend proposed to you yet?"

"Don't you start," I said with a forced smile. It wasn't a subject I was ready to discuss with anyone, not my best friend or the lodge owner.

"Sorry I asked," Shelly added quickly. "I didn't realize that it was a sore subject."

"It's not," I said. "It's just complicated."

"He loves you," Shelly said. "You clearly love him. I just don't get it. You think you have all the time in the world, but you don't. Trust me, I know from experience that you have to grab life by the horns and not let go."

"I'm sorry you lost Chester," I said sympathetically.

"Do you know what I'm sorry for? That I didn't say yes when he asked me to marry him six months ago."

It was my turn to nearly drop my own plate. "Chester proposed to you? I didn't know."

"No one was supposed to, not even Phillip," Shelly said with a shrug.

"Why did you turn him down?" Grace asked her, a question I was wondering about myself.

"I wasn't positive that he was truly finished with Maggie, so I wanted to wait until he retired so I could get him as far away from her as I could manage," she said. "How silly was that of me? Now I've lost him forever."

As Shelly started to cry, I did my best to comfort her. No one doubted that Chester would be dead now regardless of his marital status, but she did have a point. What *were* we waiting for? Once we were free of our current predicament, it might be time to finally talk to Jake about our future.

But it just wasn't the right moment now.

Grace interrupted my thoughts by asking Shelly, "Are you saying that you knew about him fooling around with Maggie all along?"

The lodge owner just shrugged. "I knew about it, but that doesn't mean that I liked it. The two of them both swore to me that it was over, but I could never be sure, you know? In the end, I finally decided that it wasn't worth fighting about."

I had to wonder if infidelity wasn't worth an argument, then what was? Then again, it was her life, not mine. The moment I'd discovered that my husband had cheated on me, I'd kicked him to the curb, but I knew that everyone was different.

Grace apparently wasn't so accepting, either. "You're kidding, right? You just put up with it?"

"It's not as clear-cut as it may sound. I'm getting older every day," Shelly said. "Besides, we all have flaws."

"Maybe so, but that's a pretty hard one to swallow," my best friend said.

"Live to be a lonely old woman my age and then we'll talk about it," Shelly said ruefully.

"I'm sorry, but I can't believe that's going to matter," Grace said. "I'd rather be alone than with someone who would do that to me."

I wasn't surprised by my best friend's opinion, though I was caught off guard by her willingness, even eagerness, to share it with us.

"Then we're just different that way," Shelly said, clearly not willing to or interested in justifying her position any further. "I used to see the world in black and white, but the older I get, the grayer everything around me becomes."

I wasn't sure how Grace would react to that, but she must have been finished with the discussion, because she just shrugged as she went back to her sandwich construction.

We didn't talk about it anymore, but then again, we didn't have to.

Once we were all gathered in the living area again, I handed Jake his sandwich.

"Thanks," he said as he took it from me. He must

have noticed something in my eyes, though, because he asked me softly, "Is everything all right?"

"It's fine," I said.

"Suzanne," he prompted.

I did my best to offer him my brightest smile. "This is the wrong time and place for this particular conversation. How about a rain check?"

Just as I asked the question, there was another flash of lightning, accompanied almost immediately by a pretty impressive explosion just outside.

"Whew. That was a close one," Kevin said.

"Everybody eat up," Jake said. "After dinner, it's time to talk."

"Are we going one on one again?" Maggie asked, clearly unhappy about the prospect.

"No, not this time. This is going to be a group discussion that involves everyone," he said.

"About what?" Nathan asked.

"What else is there to discuss? I think it's time that we all laid our cards out on the table and talked about our connections to our missing guest of honor, Chester Martin."

Chapter 22

"Sure thing," Vince said sarcastically. "Why don't you go first, Chief?"

Jake shook his head slightly. "As the leader of this little session, I think I'll reserve my comments for the end, but since you seem so eager to talk, why don't we start with you?"

Vince looked at him warily for a few seconds, and then he shrugged. "Why not? I don't have anything to hide."

"I doubt that very much," Maggie Hoff said softly, though I was pretty sure that we all heard her, which had probably been her intention all along.

"No interruptions, please," Jake said, phrasing it in the form of a request, though it was clear to everyone there that it was an order, plain and simple, and it was meant to be obeyed.

"Go on, Vince," Jake said. "Tell us about your relationship with Chester."

The man hesitated, looked at the fire for a moment, glanced over at me, and then he finally spoke. "I'm beginning to realize that the truth is probably going to come out sooner or later now that he's dead, so I might as well get it off my chest. My problems with Chester were nothing but smoke and mirrors. If anything, the guy did me a favor ten years ago by pulling out of my land deal. It took a lot of heat off me to be able to blame it on him. Maybe I milked it a little harder than I should have, but the truth of the matter is that I didn't care about him one way or the other."

"But you've been telling anyone who would listen to you for years that he cheated you," Jake said, pressing him further. It amazed me that Vince was actually repeating the story that he'd told me earlier, but I wanted to see if he continued to stick with it.

Vince looked around the darkened room as he explained, "I'm not stupid enough to incriminate myself, but I wasn't really mad at the man, and I certainly didn't kill him, and that's the truth."

"How can we be sure of that?" Shelly asked him gently.

"Just like what everyone else here says, you're going to have to take my word for it."

"What about the last time you saw him?" Jake asked. "When was it, where did it take place, and what did you say?"

"This is starting to sound more like an interrogation than I was led to believe," Vince said, and I saw a few of the others nodding in agreement.

"Think of it any way that you want to, but we're not going to get anywhere unless you all cooperate. If you have nothing to hide, you shouldn't mind answering a few simple questions."

I could almost see the wheels turning in Vince's mind, but he came to a decision with barely a pause. "Fine; if you want to play, then I'll play. It's true that I saw Chester at the library on the day that he was murdered. At least Zelda got that much right. She's your source, isn't she?"

Jake just shrugged, not confirming or denying the fact.

Vince smiled a little. "That's what I thought. Anyway, after a while, blaming Chester kind of got to be a game for me. I enjoyed watching him sweat, and I never missed a chance to tweak him. That might not make me a good person, but it doesn't make me a killer."

"So, you're admitting that you threatened Chester the day he was murdered?" I asked, forgetting my place for a moment.

"Suzanne," Jake said in warning, the way he said my name stinging a little.

"Take it easy on her," Nathan said. "It's something that I'm sure that every last one of us is thinking. Suzanne just had the courage to say it out loud."

"That's enough out of you, Nathan," Maggie said.

"Oh, blow it out your ear, Maggie," Nathan said in a simple voice that grabbed everyone's attention instantly.

"Excuse me?" Maggie Hoff asked her formerly submissive husband. "What did you just say to me?"

"You heard me, but if you'd like me to repeat it, I'd be more than happy to do it. Maggie, I've put up with a lot of garbage from you since we first got married, but I've finally reached my limit. If Chester's murder has taught me one thing, it's that life is too short to put things off that need to be done until tomorrow."

"You're going to live to regret this," Maggie said, trying to get some of her cool demeanor back.

"I doubt it, but even if you're right, this is something that I need to do for myself. From this moment on, you and I are through."

Maggie started to speak again, but instead, she just stood and moved to the other side of the room. Nathan's smile was unmistakable. He'd just proclaimed his emancipation from a bad marriage, and he clearly couldn't be happier about it. If nothing else, at least Chester's murder had given him the courage to do what he probably should have done years earlier.

"That's all well and good," Kevin said, "but let's not change the subject." He turned to look at Vince as he added, "Why are you admitting to threatening Chester the day he died?"

"I never said that I threatened him. I was just yanking his chain again, and he finally got fed up with my taunting. I knew that I'd pushed him too far this time, so I finally decided that it was time for me to back off. I told him I was through blaming him once and for all, and when I left, he was more relieved than anything else. As a matter of fact, I think he was still in some kind of shock that I was finally going to drop it."

"So you say," Kevin said.

"Think about what Zelda told you and see if it all doesn't fit," Vince told Jake. "If she told you the truth, then you'll see that I'm not lying right now."

If Jake minded this new interplay, he was keeping it to himself. Maybe he was just as fascinated by the display of human interaction as I was, or perhaps he was just trying to give the killer enough rope to hang him or herself.

Either way, I sort of wished that I had a bowl of popcorn for the exchanges.

"We only have your word that you decided to let him off the hook for something that didn't bother you in the first place," Maggie said. "I know for a fact that Chester was afraid of what you might do to him someday."

"How could you possibly know that?" Vince asked her.

"Because he told me so himself," she said.

Vince wasn't about to allow her to paint him with that particular brush, though. "I don't think pillow talk counts, sweetie."

"Watch yourself, Vince," Nathan said, clearly angered by the man's taunting words.

"Why should it bother you? I didn't think you cared about her anymore, sport."

"That doesn't mean that you can talk to her like that," Nathan said.

"Thank you, dear," Maggie said, clearly surprised by her husband's sudden rush to her defense.

"Oh, shut up, you nit. I'm not talking to you," Nathan snapped, and I let a laugh slip out before I could keep it in.

Maggie stared at me for a second with an angry intensity that was frightening before she finally broke it.

"Whether your story can be confirmed or not, I'd like to thank you for your candor," Jake told Vince.

Kevin decided to chime back in as he turned to Maggie. "You had a reason of your own to want to see him dead, didn't you? After all, he dumped you just before he was going to leave town."

I glanced over at Nathan and saw that he was fighting another outburst, and who could really blame him?

Maggie Hoff sneered at Kevin for a moment, and then she looked at Jake triumphantly. "The police chief knows that's not true. As a matter of fact, I showed him the proof of my innocence earlier today. I'm the one who ended the affair with Chester because I love my husband." The last bit she said as she looked up and stared straight at Nathan.

"I wish with all of my heart that I could believe that," he finally responded.

"You have to, dear. It's the complete and utter truth," she said.

"Don't try to sell that junk here," Shelly interjected. "For once in your life, be honest with yourself, if not the rest of us. Everybody here knows that you're a liar and an adulterer. You don't get to behave like a virtuous woman, Maggie."

"You're just jealous that Chester loved me and not you!" Maggie lashed out, the words thrusting at the lodge owner like knives.

Shelly just laughed, a reaction that I wasn't expecting. "Love? You were nothing more than a cat toy for him, something to be played with and then discarded. Spin it all you'd like, but he dumped you, plain and simple. Anything else is just a lie you keep telling yourself so you can get to sleep at night."

Maggie started to stand, her fists clenched in rage, but all it took from Jake was one command to put her in her place again.

"Don't," Jake said simply, but with enough force to drive his warning home.

"We're not finished with this, you and I," Maggie said fiercely to Shelly.

"Bring it on—any time, any place," Shelly said icily. Up until that moment, I hadn't thought her capable of murder, but now I wasn't so sure. Sure, she had an alibi, but it was an unconfirmed one at this point. If Maggie had been murdered, my money would have been on Shelly, but it was her boyfriend who had died, not the other woman, so I still wasn't sure who had done it.

"Nathan, how about you? Do you have anything to add to the conversation?" Jake asked.

The man threw his hands up in the air as he spoke. "As I said before, I didn't know about the affair until Chester was already dead, and I wasn't really positive about that until Maggie just admitted it, even after you told me about it yourself," he said wearily. The day had taken more out of him than he had, and he looked really beaten down to me. "Believe it or not, and frankly, I don't care one way or the other. I liked Chester, and I'm sad that he's dead, even if he did sleep with my wife. I just want to get out of here and start my life over."

"You don't mean that," Maggie said, her voice nearly pleading with her husband.

Nathan didn't even glance in her direction.

"Well, I certainly didn't do it," Kevin said. "Our feud was so minor, it was laughable. I wouldn't kill anyone over a million dollars, and I certainly wouldn't do it over ten bucks. Besides, our dispute was resolved once and for all, so even that petty a motive was no longer a valid one for me."

"What are you talking about?" Jake asked him.

Kevin looked truly surprised. "Didn't Suzanne tell you, or haven't you compared notes yet? I thought you two were working on this case together. No matter. I've got the proof right here." Chester again pulled out his wallet and handed the signed bill to Jake. "I'm going to be needing that back."

"Hang on a second," I said, and then I took the bill from Jake and showed the signature to Shelly. "Does that look legit to you?"

She glanced at it and then looked at me. "That's Chester's signature. There's no doubt about it in my mind."

"How can you be so sure?" Grace asked. "After all, it could be a forgery."

"But it's not," Kevin insisted.

"He's right," Shelly replied. "Chester had an odd way of signing his name, one that would be extremely tough to duplicate."

"I told you," Kevin said as he snatched it away and tucked it back into his wallet. "There, I'm free from suspicion now."

"I don't know about that," Vince snapped.

"But I just showed you all the proof!" he protested petulantly.

Vince was clearly not all that impressed. "Just because it might be hard to forge his signature doesn't mean that it was impossible. Those two things are worlds apart."

"What do you want from me, a signed absolution from the murder victim?" Kevin asked.

"That would probably do it, so unless you're able to produce it, you stay on my list," he answered.

"Is that the way you feel, too?" Kevin asked Jake.

"I'm reserving comment until the end, remember?" he asked. "Now, who does that leave on our list who hasn't spoken?"

"How about her? She hasn't said anything," Maggie said as she pointed to Shelly.

"I'm in the clear. I have an alibi," the lodge owner said smugly.

"Unconfirmed as of yet," Jake said curtly.

"Do you mean to tell me that I'm still a suspect?

You've got to be kidding me," Shelly said. "I never would have allowed this to happen if I'd known you felt that way."

"All you had to do was ask," Jake said.

It was Shelly's turn to show some outrage. As she stood, the lodge owner said, "I'll tell you one thing. I'm not going to sit in my own establishment and listen to this."

"As a matter of fact, that's exactly what you're going to do," Jake said. I glanced over and saw that he had his hand on his weapon. There was no mistaking his intent.

Shelly slumped back down in her chair, but she wasn't very happy about it.

Jake wasn't finished with her yet, though. "Are you going to tell them, or should I?"

"What are you talking about?" she asked.

"I'm talking about his will," Jake said.

Shelly shook her head. "That's nothing. It's barely even worth mentioning."

"I don't know about the rest of you, but I'd surely like to hear about it," Vince said. "Come on, Shelly. We all told our stories, so don't leave anything out of yours."

She huffed a little before she spoke. "Chester left me everything he owned, but before everyone gets too excited, you should know that what he had left was extremely modest. I'm not getting rich by any means, and by the time I finish paying off all of his bills, I'll be lucky if there's enough left for me to buy a nice meal out."

"Is that true?" I asked Jake.

"She gets it all," he replied.

"How much?"

"That I don't know yet. I was supposed to get an update an hour ago, but that's going to be tough to do without my cell phone."

"So then, that's one more motive for you," Maggie trumpeted.

"We're not keeping score," Shelly said.

"That's where you're wrong, because that's exactly what he's doing," Grace replied as she pointed to Jake.

"I wouldn't exactly put it that way," Jake said.

"You don't have to," Grace replied. "I did it for you."

"Are we through here?" Maggie asked curtly.

"There's just one more thing I'd like to know," Jake said. "Did any of you happen to send Chester a postcard?"

"What are you talking about now?" Shelly asked him incredulously. "What could that possibly matter?"

"What was on the card?" Vince asked. "Did someone say something incriminating?"

"I want to see it," Maggie said as she spoke up.

Nathan just shook his head. He was slumped down in his chair, and I had to wonder where his thoughts were.

"It was a photograph of a fire," Jake said.

There were denials all around, and my boyfriend just shrugged. "Okay, that's all that I've got for you." He glanced at his watch, and then he said, "It's getting late, so I suggest that you all get a good night's sleep. I have a feeling that tomorrow is going to bring its own set of unique problems."

"Because today was so much fun," Vince said sarcastically.

"I need my own room," Nathan told Shelly. "Do you have anything available? I can sleep out here on the couch if I need to."

"Don't be ridiculous," Maggie said. "You're staying with me."

"No, I'm not," he said gruffly to her, and then turned back to Shelly. "Do you?"

"I've got a key for one of my spare rooms right here," she said.

"You still have to come to our room to get your things," Maggie said triumphantly.

"There's nothing there I need anymore," Nathan said, and then he walked down the hallway and slipped into his new room.

Maggie stood there watching him and actually stamped her foot before she retired to her own space, and in short order, Vince and Kevin went to their respective rooms as well. Shelly headed for the upstairs to retreat to her own room when Jake spoke. "You have another empty room available, don't you?"

"Yes, why?"

"I thought so. That's where you should stay tonight," Jake said.

"Nonsense. I'll be in my own room if you need me."

Jake let her take two steps toward the kitchen hallway before he said, "Don't you realize that the killer knows that, too?"

Shelly faltered, and then she stopped dead in her tracks. After a moment, she went quietly to the desk, drew the last free key, and then she walked to her room, not speaking the entire time and slamming her door when she got into her temporary quarters.

"I don't think she's very happy with you," Grace

said with a smile.

"She'll have to get in line," Jake said, returning her grin with one of his own. "You two need to go get some sleep."

"Aren't you coming?" I asked him.

"Not tonight. I'm going to be out here on guard duty," Jake said.

"But you're exhausted. You need your sleep more than anyone does," I said.

He just shrugged. "Tonight it can't be helped."

"Let me at least stay up with you, then," I suggested.

"Suzanne, you need sleep, too."

"Not as much as you do. Besides, I'll be wide awake at one AM, and we both know it. At least let me relieve you then."

"I'm not going to put you in danger like that," Jake said.

I grinned at him as I said, "Well, we all know that it's a little too late for that."

"I'll get up with her so there will be two of us," Grace volunteered.

I turned to my best friend and said, "As much as I appreciate the offer, we both know that you're not used to being up at that hour of the night."

"So I'll make an exception," Grace said. "What do you say, Jake?"

He thought about it for a few seconds, and then he nodded. "Come relieve me at one and then we'll talk."

"Thanks," I said. I kissed him on the cheek, and then Grace and I headed to our respective rooms. It was a pretty big concession for him to make, and I wasn't going to let him down. I had to grab a few hours' sleep before I was on again, and I meant to take full advantage of it.

I never got the chance to, though.

Before my time working guard duty could begin, the world exploded all around me and shattered every last one of all of our good intentions.

Chapter 23

The first thing that woke me was the smell of smoke.

As I was climbing out of bed, I heard a woman's scream.

Not the best way in the world to wake up from a sound sleep.

I threw on my jeans and T-shirt, not even stopping long enough to put my tennis shoes on.

Maggie was in the hallway directly in front of my room when I ran outside. "What's going on, Maggie?"

"The lodge is on fire!" she screamed. "Nathan, come on! Answer the door!" Maggie pleaded as she continued to bang on her husband's door. She really must have loved him, because instead of escaping, she was staying behind to make sure that her husband was safe. I could certainly empathize with the idea of trying to save someone I loved.

"Have you seen Jake?" I asked frantically as I glanced toward the lobby and saw flames starting to lick their way up the walls toward us. I knew that he would never leave the others to fend for themselves. Was he somewhere that I couldn't see, trying to fight the fire single-handedly?

"I don't know, and I don't care!" Maggie snapped. "I need my husband!"

Nathan's door finally opened, and from his disheveled look, it was clear that he had just awoken, despite the smoke, the scream, and the banging on his door. "What's going on, Maggie? Is that smoke I smell?"

"The lodge is on fire! Come on. We need to get

out!"

"Let me grab my shoes first," he said.

"Hurry. I don't know how much time we've got!"

"We should make sure everyone else is awake before any of us leave," I said as I started banging on the other doors, starting with Grace's.

I knew that she was a sound sleeper, but this was ridiculous. When she finally answered, she was rubbing her eyes vigorously. "Suzanne, is there a fire?"

"The whole place is burning down!" I said.

"Where's Jake?" she asked as she looked wildly around. That was just one more reason that I loved her so much. She knew more than anybody how much he meant to me.

"I don't know. I can't find him anywhere!"

"I'll help you look," she volunteered, despite the danger that she would be putting herself in.

"What's all the shouting about?" Shelly asked as she came out of her room, clearly bewildered by what was happening to her business and her home.

"Can't you smell the smoke? Your lobby's on fire!"

"Has everyone gotten out?" Shelly asked.

"I don't know. I'm still looking for Jake!" I said frantically.

"Come on. I'll help," she said, and then she turned to everyone else still there in the hallway. "Let's go, people. Jake could be in trouble. He might need us."

Grace nodded, but no one else in the group seemed all that eager to help us.

"That's too bad, because he's on his own now," Vince said as he turned away from the growing flames and headed straight for the nearest exit. "It's every man for himself as far as I'm concerned."

"Kevin?" I asked. "How about you? Will you help us look?"

"Sorry," he said as he joined Vince in the exodus, "but I have to get out of here. I'm terrified of fire."

"Will you two help us?" Shelly asked Nathan and Maggie even as they started for the exit together.

"We can't do anything to help him now," Maggie said as she took her husband's hand in hers. "We have to save ourselves. Come on, honey."

In his groggy state of mind, Nathan allowed himself to be led away from the flames by his estranged wife.

Shelly did her best to smile when it was just down to the three of us. "It looks like we're it."

"You and Grace don't have to help," I told her. "You should both save yourselves."

"Not until we find Jake," Grace said firmly, and Shelly nodded in agreement. I suddenly had new respect for both women. I understood Grace's reaction, but Shelly was going down with her lodge, and no one was going to die on her watch if she could help it.

"Let's go, then," I told them, and then we started toward the flames.

"Jake! Jake!" I kept searching through the flames for any sign of him, but I didn't have any idea of where he might be. Was he somewhere else in the building, trapped under something, unable to move as the fire advanced toward him? Why wasn't he answering? Was he unconscious from the smoke? Worse yet, was he already dead?

I drove all of those thoughts from my mind. I had to move forward with the belief that Jake was okay.

It was the only way that I didn't die myself right

then and there.

"You two go that way. I'm going to check the kitchen," Shelly said.

I looked at the kitchen door and saw that it was blackened from the heat. "You can't do that. It's not safe in there."

"I'll be okay," Shelly said, but as she opened the door, a wave of smoke and flame shot out, as though it had been contained, though just barely. Grace and I managed to grab Shelly before she fell. I don't know how we did it, but we somehow managed to drag her down the hallway to the outside. It was pitch black out there now and the icy rain was coming down harder than it had yet, but it was a welcome relief from what I'd just experienced.

The group of survivors had been huddling under a nearby tree looking for some protection from the storm, but when we brought Shelly out, they broke away from their shelter and rushed to us. "What happened to her?" Maggie asked.

"She got hit with a wave of smoke and flame," I said as I turned her over to the others and headed back inside.

Grace, coughing violently from the smoke, was right beside me.

"Where do you two idiots think you're going?" Vince asked me incredulously.

"Jake's still in there," I answered resolutely.

"If you go back in there, you'll both die," Kevin pleaded.

"Maybe so, but if I live and he dies because I was afraid to go in after him, how will I ever be able to live with myself?"

Grace tried to go with me, but I couldn't allow that.

"You need to stay here," I ordered her.

"I can help," she said even as the coughing fits now doubled her over.

I took her hands in mine when she straightened up and said, "Grace, I love you like a sister, but if you go in there with me, you're just going to slow me down. I need to do this alone; do you understand me?"

"I can't let you go," she said, tears streaming down her face making tracks in the soot on her cheeks.

"You have to," I said. "For Jake's sake."

"Just be careful," she said, and then she started coughing again.

"You know it. Don't worry; I'll be back before you know it."

I opened the lodge door, felt the wave of heat and smoke hit me like a closed fist, and then I got as low as I could manage and crawled forward.

If Jake was still in there, I was going to find him.

Or die trying.

Chapter 24

The fire was a living, breathing thing now. It felt as though it was reaching out to me, trying to knock me out, but I wasn't going to let it win. Crawling carefully now, I made my way forward, inching my way closer to the flames when every fiber of my being was shouting at me to go the other way. How did firefighters do it? I was finally even with the door that led to the storm shelter, and I let my hand rest on it for one second. There was a bookcase leaning against it, but I managed to prop it up enough to get to the door, though its base was still precariously poised, ready to fall at any moment.

To my surprise, the door was cool to the touch.

That had to mean that the flames hadn't reached there yet.

Opening it slightly, I peered inside into the darkness, but I couldn't see a thing down there.

I could hear something, though, a sound that was heavenly to my ears.

"Suzanne," a voice called out in a soft whisper. "Is that you?"

"Hang on, Jake. I'm coming," I said, and I started down the steps toward him.

I was nearly there when the door slammed shut behind me. Evidently the bookcase had shifted again. There was no doubt in my mind that it was blocking the door, but that wasn't my problem at the moment.

Jake and I might be cut off from the fire for the moment, and I had no idea what other nightmares we'd face before the night was over, but we were together at last, and that was the only one thing that really mattered.

Whatever was in store for us, at least we'd face it together.

Chapter 25

I felt the water on my legs before I got to him. "Jake? Are you okay?"

"I'm just dandy," I heard him say a foot farther down the stairs.

I splashed down and found him clinging to the handrail. The water was picking up, and I could feel the current moving against me as I struggled to reach him. "What happened?"

"I heard a noise down here, so I decided to investigate. As I leaned forward at the doorway, somebody pushed me and shut the door behind me. I must have hit my head on something, because when I woke up, I heard you calling my name." After a moment's pause, he added, "Whoever did it must have taken my gun while I was out cold."

"I'm so sorry," I said as I took his head in my hands.

"Why? Are you the one who shoved me?" he asked with a hint of laughter in his voice.

"Of course not. I'm just sorry that I wasn't here for you."

"You're here now," he said, and then he paused for a moment. "Is that smoke I smell?"

"The lodge is burning down all around us," I said calmly.

"Ha ha, very funny," Jake said, and then he stopped a moment before speaking again. "Hang on. You're not kidding, are you?"

"I'm deadly serious," I said. "At least the flames haven't gotten down here yet."

"Maybe not, but we're still in trouble."

"Don't you worry. We'll find a way to get through this," I said. "Can you stand up?"

I felt him try, but he slumped back down a moment after nearly making it. "I need a minute."

"Take all the time you need," I said, trying to keep the panic out of my voice.

"Suzanne, we don't have that long until we're both going to be in serious trouble. The water level is rising at an alarming rate," Jake reported matter-of-factly. "It's coming up fast now that the main room below us has been flooded."

"I know; I can feel it moving against my legs," I replied, not getting the significance of it.

"The ceiling's sloped here, so it won't be long now until this entire space is under water," he said. "I've got to find a way to get up those stairs."

"Put your arm around me. I can help you do it."

Somehow we made it to the top, but as I pushed against the door, it wouldn't budge. That bookcase was wedged in so tightly that I wasn't sure it would ever move, at least until it burned with the rest of the lodge above us.

"Surely the water will leak around the door enough to save us," I said.

"Not at a rate fast enough to do us any good. If the water doesn't get us, then the fire surely will." He sounded almost tranquil about the situation, as though he'd already accepted our fate.

"I'm not giving up yet," I said. "Are you okay standing up on your own? If you can lean against the wall for a second, I want to try something. If I shove hard enough, I might be able to get that door open after all."

"Hang on. I'll give you a hand," he said.

"You need to stay right where you are," I cautioned him, but he managed to work himself toward the door after all.

"If we go down, we'll do it together," he said.

Working together, we put all of our combined force behind one last push that I hoped would free us, even though it meant that it would send us out directly into the roaring fire.

It wouldn't budge, though. Despite our best efforts, we were trapped.

"This is my all fault, Jake," I said sadly as I slumped with my back against the jammed door.

"How can you possibly take the blame for what's happening to us?" he asked.

"I don't mean being down here, I'm talking about being trapped. A bookcase was wedged against the door when I found you, and I didn't move it far enough away when I slipped inside. It must have shifted again when I struggled in, and it ended up trapping us." I was crying now as I spoke, but I barely noticed the tears.

"Suzanne, you found me. That's all that counts." A minuscule amount of light was coming in from the door frame, and I could just barely make out Jake's face in the faded illumination. I saw him smile a little, and then he said, "Let's try it again and see if we can move it together."

As hard as we tried, though, as much as we struggled to open that door, in the end, we both realized that we just couldn't do it.

It seemed to be that, despite our best efforts, we were both going to die tonight.

"Well, it appears that we're not going anywhere," Jake said with calm resolution. "What should we do in the meantime?" he asked as he joined me as I leaned my back against the door.

"We could spend our time trying to figure out who the real killer is," I suggested.

"Seriously, Suzanne? That's how you want to spend your last moments on earth?"

"Solving a murder with the man I love sounds like the perfect way to go out to me," I answered him, and as I said it, I realized that it was true.

"Then by all means, let's see what we've got. Why don't you go first?"

"Well, I'm afraid to admit that this time I don't have nearly as much as I'd like to have."

"You might be surprised how your information might fit in with mine," Jake said. "Besides, what else do we have to do?" I could see his grin again in the sliver of dancing yellow-and-red light still coming through the door, and I was truly happy that we'd found each other and had fallen in love, even if our time left together was going to be limited to minutes instead of decades.

"Okay," I said. "Let's start with what we all just found out this evening. Vince told me the same story earlier that he told you all in the lobby, and I believe him. He might not be a very nice man, but I don't think he's a murderer."

"Neither do I," Jake said. "He basically implicated himself in a land-fraud scheme, but he convinced me that he didn't have enough reason to kill Chester."

"Well, we know that Kevin didn't do it, either. He

showed us all that bill with Chester's signature on it, so as far as I'm concerned, he's in the clear, too."

"Agreed," Jake said. "If it's any consolation, I'm starting to feel a little better, maybe even a little stronger."

"That's good," I said, but I still didn't harbor any hope that he'd recover in time to make a difference in our situation. I wasn't sure how hard a blow to the head he'd taken in his fall, but I wasn't at all confident that he'd be able to bounce back from being concussed that quickly. "Anyway, that's all that I know. What have you got?"

"I was going to tell you in the morning, but here goes. Nathan is in the clear as well. He was booking a cruise with his travel agent at the moment Chester was murdered."

"Who still uses a travel agent?" I asked.

"It's a good thing for Nathan that he did, because he had a time-and-date-stamped receipt with him here. He was going to surprise Maggie, only the surprise was on her."

"Is that why he was holding his wallet when he walked out of your interview? I wondered about that."

Jake smiled gently at me. "You don't miss much, do you?"

"Sometimes it feels as though I don't catch anything worthwhile at all."

"Suzanne, you are much too hard on yourself."

"That's what everyone keeps telling me. I suppose that means that Maggie is the only name left on our list," I said.

"She didn't do it, either," Jake said.

"How do you know that?"

"She wasn't even in town when it happened. Maggie gave Chester an ultimatum. She told him to skip his party and go to Charlotte to their favorite hotel to meet her, or she would never speak to him again."

"But he'd already broken up with her," I said as I moved closer. The water was freezing, and I felt the chill racing through me as it climbed higher and higher up my body.

"She thought he was bluffing, but when he didn't show up, she knew that he was truly through with her. She raced back to April Springs to confront him, and she got a speeding ticket along the way. It gave her a solid alibi, so we have to take her name off the list."

"If she had an alibi, why didn't she give it to you before?"

"Suzanne, she didn't want to have to explain to Nathan what she'd been up to. She knew she would be cleared if it came down to it, so she decided to sit on the information until she really needed it, which she finally shared with me."

"I saw her tucking something into her purse when she walked out of the dining room after your interrogation. It looked like a parking ticket to me."

"Close enough," Jake said. "It gives her an irrefutable alibi."

"So, that just leaves Shelly," I said.

"That's my guess as well," Jake replied.

"How did she ever think that she could just make up an alibi and get away with it?"

"I don't think she's been planning very far beyond just not getting caught immediately. When I started checking her story out on the phone, I couldn't get confirmation of it from anyone, including the one member of her staff that I managed to speak with. Don't you think that it was kind of convenient for her that she sent them away before we all got here? There was no way that I could interrogate any of them if they weren't at the lodge."

"But she didn't know we were coming until after she sent them all away," I pointed out.

"It didn't matter if you and your gang of suspects were headed this way or not. I'd already made arrangements to visit here on my own so I could interview them all in person. I'm sure that your plan to host the other suspects here was just wonderful luck for her."

"How do you read it that way?"

Jake shivered a little, and I held him closer. "Suzanne, she knew that I was breathing down her neck, so she had three choices: she could run, she could try to get rid of me before I told anyone else about my suspicions, or she could offer me a scapegoat. The only thing that she *wasn't* counting on was the weather locking us all here. I'm guessing that she's used that as well by starting the fire."

"She burned down her own lodge?" I asked, more shocked by the implication than I was at the prospect of her being a cold-blooded killer.

"You heard her say it herself. With the flood, she knew that she was finished, and I can easily see her starting the fire for the insurance payout, as well as the prospect of getting rid of me in the bargain. That money, along with whatever Chester left her, might have just been enough for a fresh start somewhere else."

"If all that is true, then why did she volunteer to help

me look for you?" I asked him, still having a hard time accepting the fact that this woman had been so cavalier with everyone else's lives.

Jake breathed in deeply, and then he replied, "My guess is that she just wanted to make sure that I was really dead. If the fall didn't kill me, she was probably going to shoot me with my own gun."

"So, that's that. We figured it all out, but not before it could do us any good."

"At least we've got that much," Jake said.

"We have more than that," I said. "We have each other, and that's really all that matters to me."

"Right back at you," he said, and then he kissed me.

I couldn't say with any level of certainty if it actually raised my temperature or not, but it did do a world of good for my spirits. It felt wonderful knowing that together, we made a formidable team, even if we were close to the end.

If I had to go, I wanted it to be like this, with Jake beside me.

Chapter 26

"Now that we've got that settled, there's something that I've been meaning to ask you," Jake said as we leaned our backs against the jammed door. The water was up to our waists now and increasing at an impressive rate. Some water was probably leaking out around the door's edges, but Jake had been right. It wouldn't be enough to save us. If I had to guess, I'd say that we literally had just a few minutes left to live.

"Now's the time to ask, then," I said, trying to keep my tone light. This might be the end of me, but I was not going to let it define my last moments. I'd taken life head on at every opportunity in my past, and if I were meant to die tonight, then at least I'd face it on my own terms.

"Hang on. It's here somewhere," he said as I watched him pat his pockets, obviously searching for something.

"Take your time. I'm not going anywhere," I answered. Gallows humor seemed to be my go-to position in my final minutes of life.

"Here it is," he said as he retrieved something from the front pocket of his jeans. "Suzanne, I've been wanting to do this for a long time. I love you. When I lost my wife and the baby she was carrying, I never thought that I'd be able to love again, but you've shown me that my life wasn't over, and for that, I'll be eternally grateful to you."

"Jake, what are you saying?"

"Something that I should have said months ago." He started to go down on one knee, but with the rising water, it was nearly impossible. Still, I had to give him points for trying. "Suzanne, will you marry me?"

I couldn't believe it. Jake's timing was impeccable, but there was no doubt in my mind that the proposal was sincere. "You're not just asking me because it looks as though we're about to die, are you?"

"Honestly, I was going to ask you anyway," he said. "Why do you think I brought the ring with me up here? I don't mean to rush you, but the water's forcing my hand. What do you say?"

"I would be honored," I said, crying again as he slipped the ring onto my finger. It felt right there, as though my hand had been incomplete without it before. I didn't worry about Jake's past sorrows or even my bad marriage to Max. All I could think about what that this man loved me and wanted to spend the rest of his life with me, even if it could be measured by the sweeping second hand of a clock.

"Yes. Of course I'll marry you," I said.

I kissed him, but he broke it off quickly.

"What's wrong?"

"Not a thing in the world," he said with new enthusiasm. "Now that you've said yes, I've got a brand new reason to get us both out of here alive before you can change your mind."

"It's not happening, mister. You're stuck with me now, forever and always."

"How about we see if we can stretch that out a little then, shall we?" he asked as he began attacking the door with renewed vigor.

Chapter 27

Whether it was the added water pressure against the door or the fact that Jake and I now had something new to live for, I was amazed and delighted when the door finally started to budge under our dual efforts. Once it was open a touch, the force of the water shoved it the rest of the way open, sending us both to the floor of the lodge in a mass of water.

Our troubles weren't over yet, though.

We were out of the flood, but now we were directly in the heart of the fire.

Chapter 28

"Stay low," Jake said, "and crawl toward the back door."

"I can't see," I said as the smoke continued to blind me. Where was the exit, and how were we supposed to find it?

"I'll go first. Grab my ankle."

"Got it," I said, and then we didn't speak again. We both needed to save our breath for the arduous journey, even if it was just a matter of feet.

It felt to me as though it took an hour, but I knew that we were only in that inferno for a scant minute before we tumbled out through the back door.

Jake had somehow managed to find our way out.

We were free of both the flood and the fire.

Now it was time to rectify things with Shelly Graham.

Chapter 29

"Where is everybody?" I asked as I looked around us. The clearing was empty, and I wondered where Grace and the others had all gone. It had finally stopped raining, but the temperature had plummeted, and I felt myself shivering uncontrollably in the cold.

"Suzanne, lower your voice. We need to speak softly now that we're back outside," Jake said as he helped me stand up again. "Are you okay?"

"Considering what we've just been through, overall I feel like I'm doing pretty well," I said. As I brushed at the mud on my jeans, I felt my engagement ring catch on the denim fabric. "Now that we're alive, do you still want to marry me?"

"More than ever," he said fiercely. "But first we need to catch Shelly before we can celebrate."

That was all I needed to hear. I started hurrying into the darkness, ready to tackle the woman with my bare hands if I had to.

"Hang on a second," Jake said as we managed to stumble a few steps from the lodge. There was enough light from the fire to show us the world outside in shades of red and yellow, casting an eerie glow over everything around us.

"What are we waiting for?" I asked him. "We have to help Grace." The crackling sounds of the fire were getting closer, and it seemed that the old lodge was about to be completely consumed at any moment. It was ironic that I'd been praying for the rain to stop all day, and now, when we needed it the most, it had completely disappeared. The fire was burning unchecked now, consuming everything within its reach.

"I need a weapon in my hands before we do this," Jake said as he looked around to see what he might be able to improvise. "She's armed with my handgun, remember?" After a few moments, he bent down and picked something up off the ground. In the growing light from the fire, I could see that it was a plank of wood as big as a bath towel, charred completely on one end.

"What is that?"

Jake peered at it in the dim light. "It must be from the lodge. It says 'STORM' on it, and that's exactly what it's going to bring down on Shelly for trying to kill us."

"To be fair, she only tried to kill you," I said as I corrected him. Even as I spoke, I wondered about why I was arguing semantics at a moment like this.

"Maybe so, but how long do you think it would have taken her to set her sights on you?"

The idea of Shelly coming after me startled me. "Why would she want to hurt me? I was no threat to her."

"Don't underestimate yourself. You were scoring some points with your investigation, and it wasn't going to be long before she was going to perceive you as a threat. Besides, what would have happened if I had died back there and you hadn't found me in time?"

I didn't even have to think about it. "Firstly, I would never have believed that you would have let yourself be trapped like that accidently. I would have known that someone had pinned you down there. And secondly, I wouldn't have rested until I found what had really happened to you, and made the killer pay dearly for it." The thought of how close I'd come to losing Jake was scary now that we were out of the water and the fire. Even though I knew that we weren't out of the woods yet, I was starting to like our chances. After all, Shelly had to be feeling pretty good about her plan right about now. She had no idea that her efforts to kill Jake had failed, and in the interim, we'd figured out that she was Chester's killer.

Jake just smiled. "You would have continued to be a real threat to her to the point where she would have had to get rid of you sooner rather than later."

"I suppose you're right," I said. "Now that you have your weapon, are you ready to go after her?"

"Let's not burn another second," Jake said as he started off into the darkness.

I wasn't crazy about his choice of words, but I loved the sentiment.

At last, we were going to take action and do something about the seemingly calm older woman who had turned out to be a crazed killer.

Chapter 30

"I just hope that no one else is dead," I said as we were walking when Jake shushed me.

He pointed to a nearby clearing, and I could see Shelly holding the rest of them at gunpoint, including Grace. It appeared that they had been talking for quite a while. Why was she waiting to get rid of them? Was she playing some kind of cruel cat-and-mouse game, or was she simply working up her nerve to shoot them all in cold blood? Either way, it appeared that our window was closing quickly.

If we were going to save the others, we had to stop her, and fast.

"That's enough talk," we heard Shelly say as we approached the group. Jake motioned for me to stop where I was, but I shook my head and continued for a few more steps alongside him. The clouds had finally broken, and half a moon allowed us to see well enough around us to act.

Jake scowled as he pointed one finger to the ground, but again, I refused to stand idly by while my best friend's life was being threatened, and I certainly wasn't going to wait on the sidelines while Jake fought my battle for me. If my fiancé was going to put his life at risk, then so was I. I understood that I lacked his specialized training, but then again, I wasn't exactly helpless. After all, attacking an armed killer with a piece of wood was too risky to even think about, and if I could increase his odds of success even by a little bit by being a distraction, then I was going to do it.

"But I thought you had an alibi," Grace said, demanding an answer. She might be about to die, but she wasn't going to go without at least knowing the truth.

"I made it all up. So sue me," Shelly snapped. "When I got to the library, I parked around the corner and used the back entrance so we could have a little privacy before everything got started downstairs. It was mostly pure luck that nobody saw me go in or out. Chester had told me that he wanted to talk to me before the celebration, and I actually thought he was going to propose! He tried to dump me instead, so I took his favorite knife that he was going to use to cut the cake and I used it on him instead. He wasn't going to get away with throwing me away like that. I wasn't going to let myself be humiliated by a clown!"

"Hang on a second," Grace said to Shelly belligerently. "I want to know if you were the one who sent him that postcard."

"Yes, it was me, not that it did any good. I don't even think he could help himself. I suppose once a fool, always a fool." Shelly took in a deep breath, and then she added, "There's no use postponing it any longer."

"Who are you going to shoot first, Shelly?" I heard Grace ask, obviously taunting her. "You don't have the guts to do it face to face, do you? That's why you keep talking. It's a little different when it's premeditated, isn't it? Sure, you stabbed your boyfriend in the chest, but after all, he'd cheated on you. You don't have any reason to kill any of us except to protect your precious freedom. I for one don't think that you can do it."

What was she doing, *daring* Shelly to shoot her? I wasn't sure, but I thought that just maybe Grace was trying to provoke the killer enough so that she could make her own move. I was proud of her bravery, but I hoped that she didn't get herself killed before Jake and I could intervene.

"Shut up, Grace, or you'll be first," Shelly said in a growling voice. The gun moved toward my best friend, and I felt my entire body go rigid. Was Shelly about to shoot Grace? At the last second, her aim moved away though, this time straight at Maggie Hoff. "Now that you mention it, there is somebody here who deserves this more than the others," Shelly said fiercely, and then I saw her hand tense as she pulled the trigger.

For the next few seconds, everything seemed to happen in slow motion.

Nathan shoved his wife to one side even as he took the bullet meant for her. I couldn't see where it hit him, but he crumpled to the ground like a rag doll, so I knew that it was serious.

Jake leapt forward at that moment, and I'm proud to say that I was right beside him. It added another level of warmth to my heart seeing Grace attack the killer from the front even as we sprang at her. From behind, I hit Shelly's legs as Jake swung the burned sign at her head, all of this happening while Grace was two steps away. When I hit Shelly, her arm flew up, and Jake knocked the gun away, though I suspected that he'd been aiming for her head. Shelly went down in a heap, and the gun went flying into the darkness.

Jake hurried to recover his weapon as Grace and I

moved toward Nathan, still lying on the ground. Maggie had pulled his head into her lap, and she was sobbing uncontrollably. Kevin stood there in shock, and Vince almost instinctually moved behind him, as though putting space between himself and everyone else. Was he actually trying to use the man as a human shield even after the killer had been disarmed?

Jake finally came up with the gun, but when I turned back to where Shelly had just been, I saw that she was now gone.

I realized too late that I should have stayed with her, and my mistake had allowed her to escape.

Chapter 31

"How is he doing?" I asked as Grace and I knelt down beside Maggie and Nathan.

"Well, at least he's still breathing," she said as she pressed both hands against his chest.

"Hold on, Nathan," I said as I patted his head, but he only managed a moan in response.

"We have to get him some help!" Maggie pleaded.

"I'll go," Jake said as I stood up. He tried to hand me his weapon, but I just stared at it. "Suzanne, be ready in case Shelly comes back."

"What are you going to do?" I asked him, still refusing to take his firearm.

"What else can I do? I'm going to cross the stream and go for help," he said firmly.

"Jake, don't go. It's not safe," I pleaded with him.

My boyfriend—no, my fiancé—stroked my head lightly. "If I don't at least try, a man might die. I have to do this."

"Then I'm going with you," I said. "Grace, you take the gun."

She made no move to grab it, either. I knew that my offer didn't make any sense, but I didn't care. It had taken Jake and me so long to finally get together that I wasn't going to let him leave me now.

"Would *someone* please go?" Maggie asked through her tears. "I can't afford to lose him."

It amazed me how much she really seemed to care about her husband now that he might be dying. Clearly Maggie had taken him for granted all those years, but now that she was about to lose him, she was hanging onto him with everything that she had.

"Don't worry about me. I'll be back soon," Jake said as he stood.

I was about to protest once more when I heard something overhead over the roaring noise of the stream. In a moment, a helicopter burst into view, its spotlight blinding us with its brilliance. As it set down, I saw a man that I'd only met a few times leap out and rush toward us, his gun drawn.

Apparently Jake's boss was coming to the rescue, but his efforts were mostly too little and too late.

"How did he know that you were here?" I asked Jake as his former boss approached us.

"Ask him yourself. I told Kelly Blakemore all about my investigation yesterday, and just as a precaution, I gave Stephen Grant her contact information in case something happened to us up here. It was either that, or when Phillip and George got washed out on their way up here, one of them called to tell him that we were stranded up here with a killer."

"And he came running," I said.

"Why shouldn't he? It was the least he could do after all that I've done for him over the years," Jake replied matter-of-factly.

They loaded Nathan into the back of the chopper, but there was no room for the rest of us, including Jake's boss, after Maggie insisted that she had to be by her husband's side.

"Thanks for coming, Grafton," Jake told his former boss after the chopper took off.

"We don't leave our people behind," the man said. "I got the call, and I came running."

"The only problem with that is that I'm not your people anymore, remember?"

"We can talk about that later," Grafton said. "I'm just glad that you're okay."

Jake just shrugged, but before he could reply, we heard the chopper noises overhead again. "Why are they coming back?"

"They aren't. I brought another chopper with me," Grafton said. "There was no shortage of volunteers to come up here after you. You have a great many friends in the department."

"Well, I'll give you that much. You didn't hold anything back."

"We got here as soon as we could manage it with the storm," he said. As the other chopper landed where the last one had so recently taken off, Grafton said, "Hang on one second. I'll be right back."

Grafton rushed up to the helicopter, its blades still furiously turning, and I squeezed Jake's hand. "It's all pretty impressive, isn't it?"

Jake just shrugged. "It doesn't matter. None of it is going to change my mind."

"You can always go back to your old job, you know," I said.

Jake was about to answer me when Grafton rejoined us. "There's no longer any need to worry about the woman."

"Why is that?" I asked him.

"The pilot spotted her body coming across the stream. She got caught on a log and drowned. We'll retrieve her body at daybreak," he said as he glanced at the growing sunrise, "which should be any minute now. What do you say we get you out of here?" he asked.

"Where are we going?" I asked him.

"Just to the other side. There are some folks waiting for you over there."

"Lead the way," I said as Grace, Jake, and the rest of us followed him to the helicopter. We couldn't all jam into it, but I wasn't about to wait around for the second trip when my mother was just across the raging stream. I didn't even need confirmation that she was there.

It was as certain as the rising sun to me.

When we landed, I quickly found myself in Momma's embrace, but only for a moment. Before I knew what was happening, George added himself to the mix, and Chief Martin as well. He was truly relieved to see me, and I realized that it was about time I started calling him Phillip, if I could somehow bring myself to do it.

"Are you okay?" Momma said as she finally broke the group hug and stroked my hair. I lightly pushed some of it away after a moment.

"I'm fine," I said when my mother grabbed my hand.

"Suzanne Hart, is there something that you'd like to tell me?"

"Oh, that. Yeah, that. I'm engaged," I said with a grin.

"Congratulations," she said, which spurred another round of hugs, including Grace this time. After I finished telling them the full, dramatic story of the proposal, they descended en masse on Jake and he disappeared in a sea of well wishers.

All in all, it was a happy reunion, but I had to wonder about Nathan as I found myself being smothered in warm blankets. Would he make it, and if he did survive the gunshot wound, would he stay with Maggie after all that had happened between them?

How would the chief, er… Phillip, take the news about who had killed his brother, and why?

And how would Jake respond to the heightened pleas of his boss to rejoin him at the state police?

There were a great many questions still to be answered, but as far as I was concerned, the only crucial one had already been addressed.

Jake had asked me earlier, and my answer had been a resounding yes.

I was getting married again, and this time, I was certain that it would be forever!

And nothing else really seemed to matter beyond that.

RECIPES

Suzanne and Momma's Hot Chocolate

Some folks wonder why we go to so much trouble making our own hot chocolate mix when there are so many perfectly fine blends available at the nearest grocery store, but one sip of this and you'll never go back! This is, without a doubt, the finest hot chocolate recipe in the world, at least according to me and my family! Don't wait for a cold winter night to try this; it's just as delicious in the summertime, too.

Ingredients

2 cups powdered nonfat milk
¾ cup granulated sugar
½ cup powdered nondairy creamer
¼ cup Hershey's cocoa powder
¼ cup Hershey's special dark chocolate cocoa powder
1 dash of table salt

Warm milk, whole or 2%

Directions

Mix the powdered ingredients thoroughly and then store in a tight, covered container in the freezer until needed. For each cup of hot chocolate, add ¼ cup of the mix to ¾ cup warm milk, heated carefully over the stovetop or in the microwave until it reaches a gently warm temperature. Stir well, add a dollop of whipped or plain marshmallows if preferred, and enjoy!

Makes 3¾ cups of the mix, or 15 mugs

Momma's Apple Crisp

Apple Crisp is one of Momma's favorites, and one of ours, too! This can be made without using the crust in a casserole dish, but I like it best as a pie. Once upon a time I used Granny Smith apples exclusively, but lately I've been mixing a few Staymen, Winesap, or Pink Ladies into the mix. My ratio is two Granny Smiths for every other apple. These pies will wake a sleeping teenager when they're baking—a rare feat indeed!

Ingredients

An 8- or 9-inch pie crust, premade or a homemade crust, if preferred

Filling
5 to 6 cups thinly sliced firm, tart apples (Granny Smiths work well as the base, with a few Staymen, Winesap, or Pink Ladies to balance the tartness)
½ cup granulated sugar
3 tablespoons white all-purpose unbleached flour
½ teaspoon cinnamon
½ teaspoon nutmeg
A dash of salt

Crisp Topping
1 cup white all-purpose unbleached flour
½ cup dark brown sugar
½ cup butter, cubed and at room temperature

Directions

Peel and core all of the apples, then cut them into thin slices. In a large bowl, mix the apple slices together thoroughly to evenly distribute the different kinds of apples in the pie. Next, in a smaller bowl, sift together the sugar, flour, cinnamon, nutmeg, and salt, then stir the dry mixture into the apple slices until they are evenly coated. Add the apple slices to the pie shell. Then, in another bowl, combine the flour and brown sugar, then cut in the butter with a fork or a pastry cutter. The mix should be crumbly and formed into small chunks the size of lima beans to peas. Add this mixture on top of the apples. Then bake the pie uncovered in a 425° F oven for 30 to 45 minutes, until the crust is golden brown and a butter knife slips into the pie easily. Cool the pie as long as you can stand it, but if you want a bite when it's fresh out of the oven, be prepared for a deluge of lovely, sweet juices from the slice.

Momma's Pot Roast

We make pot roast much the way Momma does in the donut shop books, using a slow cooker to let the meat and veggies cook long and slow. The smells that waft through the house are absolutely incredible, and I'm always hungry well before the meal is ready! It's worth the wait, though. If you watch for appropriate meat cuts to go on sale, this is an extremely economical meal, and delicious to boot!

Ingredients

2 tablespoons canola oil
2 tablespoons all-purpose unbleached flour
1/8 teaspoon salt
1/8 teaspoon pepper
1 boneless beef chuck roast, 2 to 2½ pounds
2 medium russet or red potatoes, peeled and cubed
carrots, baby or peeled, cut into 1-inch sections, about 1 lb.
Any good onion soup mix packet, about 1 oz.
1 cup tap water
1 tablespoon of either cornstarch, all-purpose flour, or powdered tapioca
1/3 cup cold water

Directions

Over medium heat, add the canola oil to a nonstick frying pan and warm until a drop of water sizzles when dropped into it. While you're waiting, mix the flour, salt, and pepper together, and then coat the roast with the mix. Brown the meat on all sides in the hot pan, and then drain off the fat. In the slow cooker, spray the pot with nonstick vegetable spray (or use a slow-cooker liner, which makes cleanup super easy), and then add the potatoes and carrots to the bottom of the slow cooker. Add the browned roast next, and then sprinkle the soup mix on top. Next, add the water until the veggies are almost covered, but not the roast. Put the lid on the slow cooker and cook on HIGH for 6 hours, or until the roast falls apart with gentle prodding from a fork. Remove the roast and veggies to a serving plate and cover everything with aluminum foil to keep it all warm, then strain the liquid and pour it into the pan you used to brown the meat originally. In a small bowl, add the thickening agent (cornstarch, all-purpose flour, or powdered tapioca) to the cold water, and then stir it all together in the pan, heating it at a simmer until the gravy is formed. Serve the gravy directly on the roast and carrots if you'd like, or serve separately. If you want to skip making the gravy, the meal's just fine without it! Either way, it should be delicious!

Serves 4 to 6 people, depending on serving size

Momma's Homemade Chicken Pot Pie

It's easy to see why chicken pot pie is a favorite around Momma's table, and ours, too. When we have leftover chicken, this is the go-to meal that gives it an entirely different life! You can make your own crust for this, but I like the premade refrigerator kind. They are just as tasty as mine, and a whole lot easier to use. For sides, you can't beat cranberry sauce, and some lima beans really top off the meal for my household.

Ingredients

1 cup chicken, cooked and cut up into bite-sized pieces, light, dark meat, or a mix of the two, depending on preference and availability
4 tablespoons butter, unsalted
1 box or bag of mixed vegetables of your choice, any frozen mix, about 12 to 19 oz. We use the blend with corn, peas, carrots, and green beans.
4 tablespoons unbleached all-purpose flour
2 dashes table salt
2 dashes pepper
1 1/4 cups milk (whole, 2%, or 1%)

1 pie crust, from the frozen section for a quick meal

Directions

Preheat the oven to 425° F.

While you're waiting for the oven to preheat, melt the butter over low heat in a large skillet. While the butter is melting, defrost the veggies in the microwave, and if you're using a store-bought crust, let that rest on the counter at room temperature until you're ready for it. When the butter is melted, remove the pan from the heat and add the flour, salt, and pepper, combining it all thoroughly until it's all incorporated. Put the pan back on low heat and cook this flour/butter mixture for 2 to 3 minutes, stirring repeatedly. Next, add enough milk (3 to 4 tablespoons) to the pan to make a smooth mixture. Stir this constantly, still on low heat. When the mixture is smooth, add the rest of the milk and turn the heat to high, stirring constantly now. When the first bubbles begin to form, remove the pan from the heat altogether and continue stirring. Now it's time to add the chicken and frozen veggies, mixing them all in thoroughly. Transfer the mixture into an 8- or 9-inch pie pan and cover the top with a store-bought crust (or the handmade one you made ahead of time using the directions written on the next page), pinching the edges and cutting slits in the top of the crust to let the steam escape during the baking process. Now's the time to gently wash the top of the crust with egg white for a shinier crust if you like before the pie goes into the oven.

Bake the chicken pot pie in the 425° F oven for 25 to 35 minutes, or until the crust on top is golden brown. Take it out, let it cool for five minutes, and then it's ready to serve!

Serves 4 to 6 people, depending on the serving size

Author's Note:
Sometimes I like to make my chicken pot pies in smaller, one-serving portions using bowls that are oven safe. These can be festive during the holidays, when I also tend to get a little fancier with the crusts, making lattice patterns or cutting out sections of the dough with small cookie cutters before baking.

Momma's Homemade Pie Crust

My late, truly great mother-in-law taught me how to make these crusts. As hard as I've tried, I've never gotten one to come out as wonderfully as hers, but they are still pretty tasty, and it hasn't stopped me from trying!

Ingredients

1/3 cup lard (Yes, I just wrote *lard*. If that's too much for you, grab a ready-made crust from the store. I won't tell if you won't!)
1 cup unbleached all-purpose flour
1 dash salt
3 to 4 tablespoons water

Directions

In a small bowl, work the lard into the flour/salt mixture with a fork until you've formed pea-sized pellets. Next, sprinkle in the water, one tablespoon at a time, and work that into the pastry as well. Once that's all been incorporated, add more cold water slowly in 1-teaspoon increments until the mixture pulls away from the side of the bowl and the flour is incorporated into the dough. Be careful not to add too much water too quickly, or you'll have a gooey mess on your hands. When you're happy with the results, form the pastry into a ball, and then flatten it with a rolling pin to ¼- to

½-inch thickness. It's ready to use now, but if you'd like, you can store it in a ball in the fridge for a few hours before you need to roll it out!

Hot Chocolate Delight Donuts

This donut is based on the one Suzanne created in this book. While I know that my offerings can never match hers, we like these, especially in cold weather. I just had to offer this recipe so you'd have at least one new donut to try!

Ingredients

Dry
1 cup bread flour (unbleached all-purpose flour can be used as well)
½ cup hot chocolate mix (see recipe, or use a store-bought powder)
1 teaspoon baking powder
¼ teaspoon baking soda
¼ teaspoon nutmeg
¼ teaspoon cinnamon
1/8 teaspoon salt

Wet
1 egg, beaten
½ cup chocolate milk (2% or whole preferred)
3 tablespoons butter, melted
½ cup granulated sugar
1 teaspoon vanilla extract

Directions

In a large bowl, combine the dry ingredients (flour, hot chocolate mix, baking powder, baking soda, nutmeg, cinnamon, and salt) and sift together. In a separate bowl, combine the wet ingredients (beaten egg, chocolate milk, butter, sugar, and vanilla). Slowly add the wet mix to the dry mix, stirring until it's all incorporated, but don't overmix.

Bake in the oven at 350° F for 10 to 15 minutes in cupcake trays or small donut molds. I bought a dedicated donut baker that sits on my countertop, and I absolutely love it. It's easy to use, reliable, not expensive at all, and makes perfect donuts every time. These donuts usually take 6 to 7 minutes to make.

Once the donuts are finished, remove them to a cooling rack. After they cool just a bit, they can be covered with chocolate icing or a chocolate glaze with chocolate sprinkles for an extra jolt, but actually, they are good enough to eat as they come out of the oven.

Makes 5 to 9 donuts, depending on baking method

If you enjoy Jessica Beck Mysteries and you would like to be notified when the next book is being released, please send your e-mail address to **newreleases@jessicabeckmysteries.net**.

Your e-mail address will not be shared, sold, bartered, traded, broadcast, or disclosed in any way. There will be no spam from us, just a friendly reminder when the latest book is being released.

Also, be sure to visit our website at jessicabeckmysteries.net for valuable information about Jessica's books.